BONE CHILLERS

Little Pet Shop of Horrors

Tears in her eyes, Cassie hurried out of the store. All the way home the dog's sorrowful whine echoed in her mind. The eerie feeling about the pet shop and Mr Willard grew bigger and bigger. She could see his cold smile and black watery eyes dancing in her mind.

Poor dog, *she thought*. I know he was trying to tell me something. But what?

Lions
An Imprint of HarperCollinsPublishers

BONE CHILLERS

Little Pet Shop of Horrors

Betsy Haynes

Lions
An Imprint of HarperCollinsPublishers

First published in the USA in 1994 by
HarperCollins Publishers Inc.
First published in Great Britain in Lions in 1994
1 3 5 7 9 10 8 6 4 2

Lions is an imprint of HarperCollins Children's Books,
a division of HarperCollins Publishers Ltd, 77-85 Fulham
Palace Road, Hammersmith, London W6 8JB

ISBN 0 00 675024 9

Printed and bound in Great Britain
by HarperCollins Manufacturing Ltd, Glasgow

Little Pet Shop of Horrors

For Coney, Lollipop, Maxie,
Heidi, and Duchess

Chapter

Cassidy Cavanaugh brought her bike to a skidding stop. She stared at the small red brick building. "Look at that pet shop," she said, pointing. "I don't remember seeing it before. Where'd it come from?"

Cassie and her best friend Suki Chen were out riding their bikes. It was a scorching hot summer afternoon, and they were trying to cool off.

"Me either," said Suki. "It's weird. There was an empty lot there the last time we came by."

"Yeah, that's what I thought," agreed Cassie. "But they couldn't have built a whole building in one week. And look at the vines. They're growing all the way up to the roof. Even mutant vines don't grow that fast."

Suki shrugged and flipped her straight black hair

over one shoulder. "Who cares? I'm roasting out here. Let's go back to my house and blast the air-conditioning."

Cassie shook her head and stared at the building. It looked old—really old. She wondered if maybe they'd built it with antique bricks to make it look that way.

"You just want to go home so you can practice gymnastics," she said to Suki. "I want to go check out the store. I bet they have some cute puppies in there."

It annoyed Cassie that gymnastics was practically the only thing Suki cared about. Especially since Cassie couldn't even do a decent cartwheel. Cassie was too big to be a gymnast, anyway.

All the gymnasts Cassie had ever seen were small and cute, like Suki. None of them were tall and bony like Cassie. *I need binoculars to see past my knobby knees all the way to my feet—my huge feet,* she thought.

"You know I've got to practice for that meet next Saturday," complained Suki. "It's a really big deal."

"And you know how much I love animals," said Cassie. "I want to see what they've got in that store. It'll only take a couple of minutes."

"Oh, all right," Suki said. "But I'm out of there if they have any snakes. I *hate* snakes!"

They walked their bikes to the front of the store.

It wasn't much like any pet store Cassie had seen. Usually they had big windows so that you could look inside and see all the cute, cuddly puppies and kittens. This one just had a bulletin board inside one small window. It had pictures of dogs and cats thumbtacked to it. It reminded her of the wanted posters for criminals they had in the post office.

Cassie read a sign that was posted over the bulletin board:

CUSTOM PETS
TELL US EXACTLY WHAT TYPE PET YOU'RE LOOKING
FOR, AND WE'LL FIND IT FOR YOU.
SATISFACTION GUARANTEED!!!

Suki opened the door, and Cassie followed her inside.

The walls of the store were lined with cages, but most of them were empty. A single lightbulb was hanging from the center of the ceiling. It cast a dim glow over everything, making it hard to see. Cassie walked over to check out the animals in the cages.

"This is a pretty lame pet shop," said Suki. "They really don't have much."

Only three of the cages had dogs in them. Another held two kittens.

When they saw the girls, the dogs started frantically pawing at the doors to their cages. The kit-

3

tens started meowing and walking in circles.

Cassie knelt down in front of a cage with a husky puppy inside. Its fur was soft and fluffy. "Ohhh, poor thing. He's lonely."

The husky pushed up against the door and looked up at Cassie. She stuck her fingers through the bars and scratched it on its neck.

The puppy whimpered.

"He's got the saddest eyes," Cassie cooed. "I'd love to take him home with me."

Cassie suddenly felt a tickle in the back of her nose.

"AH-AH-AH-CHOO!" Cassie sneezed. "Darn it! AH-CHOO!" she sneezed again.

"Bless you," Suki said. "With your allergies, Cassie, that puppy would probably make you sneeze yourself to death."

"Bless you!" said a voice.

Cassie rubbed her nose and turned to see who had said that.

Sitting behind the counter on a stool was a very pale and incredibly fat man. He looked like a giant bullfrog propped on a lily pad.

Cassie squinted in the dim light, trying to see the man's face.

His eyes were bulging out of their sockets. His mouth was wide and thin. He didn't seem to have lips. He was gross!

4

"Thanks," she murmured, trying to throw off the creepy feeling he gave her.

"My name is Mr. Willard. Can I help you young ladies?" he wheezed from his perch on the stool.

"No, we're just looking," said Suki. "Come on, Cassie. You promised we'd just stay a minute."

"I'm sure I can show you a pet that would interest you," said Mr. Willard. Struggling to get down off his stool, he waddled toward them. "If one of these animals isn't satisfactory, I can get you any kind of pet you want," he said. "Any kind at all."

Cassie could smell his sour breath. And she couldn't help noticing his eyes. They were solid black and watery, like a giant bug's.

Cassie heard a whine behind her and looked back at the husky puppy. Was it begging to come with her?

"Come on, Cassie. You promised," said Suki, tugging at her arm.

"Okay," Cassie answered reluctantly.

She looked over her shoulder as they left the shop. The man was staring at her with his black watery eyes.

"You'll be back," he said.

Then he laughed.

Chapter

On the way to Suki's house they passed by City Park. *I'd really rather ride my bike in the park than stay inside at Suki's. Who cares about the stupid old air-conditioning?* thought Cassie. *When you pedal fast, the breeze keeps you plenty cool.*

"Hey, David, come on! Let *me* play with it. Pleeeze!"

Cassie heard a boy's voice nearby. It sounded like some boys from her school. She and Suki stopped their bikes to see what was going on.

"As usual, David Ferrante's showing off for his friends," said Suki.

Cassie shaded her eyes from the bright sunlight. She could see David and four other boys from their class huddled in a circle. David was holding a small white box. Cassie noticed that the box had holes in its sides.

David opened the top just long enough for the others to peek inside. Then he slammed it shut.

"Come on, David. I didn't even get to see it," cried Max Neal.

"Me, either," complained Todd Cook. "Keep the lid off longer."

"Too bad. It's my turn next," said Ken Coffey, elbowing his way closer to David.

"I wonder what he's got in that box," said Cassie.

"Who cares?" said Suki, heaving a bored sigh. "Maybe it's his brains. They're certainly tiny enough to fit in that box. Let's go. I can hear the air-conditioning calling me, can't you?"

"Get serious," said Cassie. "I've got to know what's in that box. Do you think David would let us see it?"

"Ca-*aassi!*" moaned Suki. "Have you totally lost it? You know the kind of stupid jokes David Ferrante is always pulling. It's probably something disgusting."

"I know, but . . . ," said Cassie. She put her foot on the pedal to leave. Then she stopped. It really bugged her when people kept secrets from her.

David raised the lid a couple of inches, holding the box up so that Ken Coffey could peak in. The next instant he slammed the lid shut again.

"Aaaahiiieee!" Ken cried. "Totally cool! Let me

see it again! Come on, David! Let me see it!"

"Now, I've *got* to find out what's in that box," Cassie said.

She pushed down the kickstand, angled the front wheel so that the bike would stand up on its own, and marched toward the group of boys.

They were so intent on the box that none of them noticed her.

"David, can I *see*?" she asked sweetly.

David looked up and grinned. "It's Hopalong Cassidy!" he teased. "Hey, everybody, say hi to Hopalong!"

Cassie's face turned bright red with embarrassment as the boys broke into wild laughter.

Shouts of "Hi, Hopalong!" filled the air.

Cassie *hated* it when David called her Hopalong. David knew that, so he did it all the time. It was even worse when he got other kids to say it, too.

"David Ferrante, you are such a jerk!" she yelled, spinning around and heading back for her bike.

"Hey, Hopalong, where are you going?" he called. "I thought you wanted to see what's in the box?"

Cassie stopped. She knew that it was dangerous to trust David. But it was all she could do to keep from turning around.

"Come here," David coaxed. "I'll let you see, if you want to. Don't you want to *see*?"

9

"Ignore him, Cassie," Suki warned. She had parked her bike and was heading toward them.

"Come on, Suki-Pukey. You can see, too," David said.

"Listen, you jerk!" Cassie cried, angrily advancing on David. "You—"

Suddenly David held the box out toward her and took the lid completely off. It was almost under her nose. She couldn't help but look inside.

"Eeeeyuk!" Cassie squealed.

A giant tarantula was staring back at her with black beady eyes! Its long, hairy front legs waved as if it were reaching out for her.

The tarantula was lunging right at Cassie's face.

Chapter

3

"**G**et that thing away from me! Get it away!" Cassie shrieked, throwing up her hands and backing away from the boys.

She backed right into a giant tree. She couldn't escape as David shoved the box in front of her face.

Cassie stared in horror at the huge black tarantula. It stared back at her, its long legs preparing to jump.

She screamed and pressed against the tree. Her eyes bugged out, and her heart pounded in her chest.

"Stop it, you moron!" yelled Suki. "Come on, Cassie. Let's get out of here." She turned a back flip. And another. And another until she was several feet away.

Cassie wanted to run, too, but she was paralyzed with fear.

David laughed.

All around her the boys were shouting.

"Chicken!" called Ken. "Hopalong Cassidy's a chicken!"

"Yeah," yelled Todd, making clucking noises. "And Suki-Pukey's gonna puke!" He stuck a finger down his throat, belching and gagging.

"Hey, David, that's enough. Close the box, will you?" said Max. "What if she dies of fright or something?"

"Now who's a chicken?" David spat out.

Max shrugged. "You've already scared them. It's not fun anymore."

Reluctantly David closed the lid and pulled the box from under Cassie's nose.

She opened her mouth to thank Max, but he shot her a warning look before she could say anything.

"David got the tarantula at that new pet shop over there," Max said quickly. He was pointing toward the pet shop that Cassie and Suki had just come from.

"It's a really neat place," said David. "The sign in the window says they'll get you whatever kind of pet you're looking for, and they guarantee it. And that's what I did," he bragged. "I went in two days ago and told them I wanted the *biggest* and *hairiest* and *ugli-*

est tarantula they could find." He smiled. "Then this morning they called me and said they had him. Isn't he great!"

"We saw the sign," said Suki. "And we went in. It's no big deal. They don't even have many pets."

"I thought girls were supposed to be smart." David smirked. "Let me explain it to you really slowly. You tell the guy in there what you want, and he special-orders it for you," David said, taking forever.

Suki stuck her tongue out at him.

Cassie shrank back against the tree as David opened the box again.

He took the spider between two fingers, and held it over his head so everyone could see. Its legs wiggled and batted the empty air.

"I'm naming him Igor," David said, grinning slyly.

He put the tarantula on his shoulder and lurched forward, limping and dragging one foot across the grass in a perfect hunchback imitation.

"Don't do it!" said Cassie as he inched closer to her.

He had one hand raised like a claw. His face was twisted into a hideous grin.

Behind him the other boys giggled and slapped each other's backs.

"David Ferrante, you'd better not!" squealed Cassie.

Before she could move, David shouted, "And I got Igor to scare the daylights out of girls—*like this!*"

He reached up and plucked the spider off his shoulder. With a sweeping motion he pitched it at Cassie.

She heard herself shrieking at the top of her lungs as the hairy monster landed on her arm.

"Get it off! Get it off!" she cried, shaking her arm and flinging the tarantula onto the ground.

"Come on!" shouted Suki, grabbing Cassie's arm and pulling her away from the tree. "Let's get away from these idiots!"

Cassie stumbled after Suki. As she hurried toward her bike, she glanced back over her shoulder.

The boys were laughing. "Hopalong Cassidy is a chicken!" yelled one.

"Suki-Pukey is gonna puke!" shouted another.

Jumping on their bikes, the girls rode away as fast as they could.

Chapter

4

The girls parked their bikes in Suki's driveway and hurried inside to the basement playroom.

The furniture there had been pushed against the walls and the rug rolled up. A mat had been placed on the floor so that Suki could practice her tumbling routines.

Cassie sat down on a huge beanbag and watched as Suki went through her warm-up exercises. She was still furious at David Ferrante.

"I almost died when that spider landed on my arm. That David Ferrante is so stupid," she huffed.

"Tell me about it," said Suki, rolling her eyes. "If those boys call me Suki-Pukey one more time, they're going to be really sorry," she grumbled, doing the splits.

"I've never heard of a pet shop that took orders like that, have you?" Cassie asked, changing the subject.

Suki was doing walkovers now, so she was upside down. She shook her head, her hair twirling on the mat. "It sounds weird to me. What if somebody wanted a hippopotamus?"

Cassie giggled. "Or a giraffe?"

"Hey, I've got an idea," cried Suki, bouncing upright again. "We could order an anteater the next time we want to go on a picnic."

"I wonder if they'd take him back after the picnic was over," Cassie said.

"What about a tyrannosaurus?" Suki chuckled. "Maybe we could get one and sic it on David."

"Yesss!" said Cassie, punching her fist into the air.

"Or a raptor," yelled Suki. "Like in *Jurassic Park*!"

The girls broke up laughing, and Suki did three fast back flips.

Cassie grew serious again and said to Suki, "Can you believe how cute that husky puppy was? I felt so bad, seeing him locked up in a cage in that shop." Cassie sighed, remembering the puppy's pleading eyes. "My parents won't let me have a pet because of my allergies. Every time I'm around cats and dogs, I sneeze my head off. I guess my mom and dad are afraid that if we had a pet, my allergies might turn into asthma."

16

"I heard that there are certain kinds of dogs that no one is allergic to," said Suki. "I saw something about it on TV. I don't know what breed they are, but I'll bet the guy at that pet shop could tell you. Maybe he'd even order one for you. Why don't you ask him?"

A vision of Mr. Willard waddling toward her sprang into Cassie's mind. She shivered again at the memory of his fleshy, ghostly white skin and large watery eyes. And the way he smiled—it gave her the creeps.

That's ridiculous, she thought. *He's probably a really nice man.*

Jumping to her feet, she said, "Come on, let's go there right now. I want to find out what kind of dogs there are that don't make people sneeze."

Suki shook her head. "Bummer, Cassie, I'd love to, but I really need to practice for the meet on Saturday. My tumbling routine stinks, and I'm competing against Laura Carter. You know she's the best tumbler in the county."

Cassie left Suki's house a few minutes later and rode her bike back to the pet shop. Parking on the sidewalk, she stopped to read the sign once more.

CUSTOM PETS
TELL US EXACTLY WHAT TYPE PET YOU'RE LOOKING
FOR, AND WE'LL FIND IT FOR YOU.
SATISFACTION GUARANTEED!!!

Maybe . . . just maybe . . . Mr. Willard can find me a dog I won't be allergic to, Cassie thought happily. She opened the door and went inside.

The room was still dark and gloomy. Cassie noticed that it smelled bad, too. Mr. Willard was perched on his stool at the back of the store. The corners of his mouth turned up in a wide grin when he saw Cassie.

Cassie glanced at the cages and saw that the husky was gone. She was happy that the puppy found a home.

"Can I help you, miss?" Mr. Willard asked.

"I hope so," said Cassie, rubbing her nose. Another tickle was starting up.

"My friend told me that there were certain kinds of dogs that people who are allergic—ACHOO! Excuse me," she said, feeling her nose stop up. "Dogs that don't make people sneeze," she added quickly. "Do you have any?"

Mr. Willard inhaled deeply. It sounded like air escaping from a leaky balloon.

"There are a number of short-haired breeds that people with your problem can own," he wheezed.

He put his fingers together like a church steeple and peered over them at her. His black watery eyes stared directly into hers.

18

Cassie suddenly realized that Mr. Willard hadn't blinked once since they'd been talking. *That's weird,* she thought. *This whole place is weird!*

"I don't happen to have any in stock at the moment," he continued, "but if you'd care to fill out an order form, I could get one for you in a couple of days."

Cassie's heart leaped. She reached for the ballpoint pen he was handing her. Then her hand froze.

"I've got to talk to my parents first," she said, sighing. "They wouldn't like it if I ordered something without telling them. But you're sure you could get a dog that won't make me sneeze?"

The corners of his mouth turned up ever so slightly. "Absolutely. I can fill any order. Some just take more time than others. Ask your parents to call me here at the store if they want more information."

"Thanks," said Cassie. "I'll go home and talk to them right now."

She skipped toward the door, feeling happier than she had in a long time. *I might get a dog,* she sang to herself. *A cute little puppy even.*

Suddenly she heard a deep, menacing growl behind her. She whirled around in horror.

A huge black dog was coming through a door at

19

the back of the store. It let out another low, rumbling growl. Its lips were rolled back, baring long white fangs.

It was rushing straight at Cassie!

Chapter

"*GRRRRR!*"

Cassie froze as the snarling dog came bounding across the room. Its eyes were fixed on her throat. She ducked her head and threw up her arms to protect herself.

"Cuda! Halt!" shouted Mr. Willard. He grabbed the dog by its spiked collar and pulled it to a stop.

Cassie stood shaking with fear at the massive dog. It was just inches from her.

"Bad dog! Bad Cuda!" Mr. Willard scolded. He looked at Cassie with his black, unblinking eyes. "My apologies, miss. This is Barracuda. He needs a little training." He paused to catch his breath.

Cassie gulped. She knew that barracudas were mean and dangerous. That they had razor-sharp teeth that could cut you to shreds in an instant.

She shot a fearful look at Cuda's fangs.

"He's one of our custom-ordered watchdogs. His new master is on his way to pick him up," Mr. Willard wheezed. "I don't know how he got out of the back room."

Cassie's heartbeat was slowly returning to normal. She nodded and murmured, "That's . . . that's okay."

As she turned to leave, she felt a soft tap on her leg and jumped. Startled, she looked down. Cuda was reaching out a paw to get her attention. To her amazement he suddenly didn't seem vicious at all.

He whimpered softly and lay down on the floor at her feet. Wiggling to get closer, he looked up at her with huge brown eyes. He seemed to be pleading, the way the husky puppy had.

How could I have ever been afraid of him? she wondered.

"Good doggie," she said softly. She knelt beside him and stroked his head. He whimpered again and pressed closer to her. The sound he was making was strange. Almost as if he were trying to talk. "What is it, Cuda? What are you trying to tell me?" Cassie asked.

Mr. Willard jerked Cuda's collar and tried to haul the dog to its feet and away from her. "Back, Cuda! Get into the back room right now!" he ordered.

Cuda planted his back end firmly on the floor and braced himself against the pull. He looked at Cassie with wide eyes and made the funny sound, only louder this time.

"Arroaroro!"

Gripping Cuda's collar tightly, Mr. Willard huffed and puffed and began dragging the huge dog toward the back of the store.

"It's okay," Cassie insisted, following them. "I'm not afraid of him. Honest."

Mr. Willard ignored her.

Cuda looked over his shoulder and rolled his eyes back at Cassie. He let out a piteous wail. Cassie stood there, her hands over her mouth. Her heart was breaking at the awful sound. She watched the tortured dog helplessly.

"Please don't hurt him," she cried as Mr. Willard shoved Cuda through the door and slammed it.

Tears in her eyes, she hurried out of the store. All the way home the dog's sorrowful whine echoed in her mind. The eerie feeling about the pet shop and Mr. Willard grew bigger and bigger. She could see his cold smile and black watery eyes dancing in her mind.

Why had he been so mean to Cuda?

Poor Cuda, she thought. *I know he was trying desperately to tell me something. But what?*

Chapter

"Absolutely not," Cassie's father said. Cassie had asked him as soon as she got home from Custom Pets if she could get a puppy. "Those salesmen will tell you anything. All they care about is making you buy something."

"That's right, dear," said Mrs. Cavanaugh, shaking her head and frowning. "And your health is our biggest concern."

"But Dad, Mom," Cassie pleaded. "It's not just *his* word. Suki's the one who told me about dogs that are okay for people with allergies. She heard all about it on television. The dogs don't shed at all. That's what makes people sneeze," Cassie explained. She could tell that her parents weren't convinced. It was time to beg. "You know I only went to the pet shop in the first place to find out if Suki was right. And Mr. Willard said she was. Just talk to Mr. Willard. Please. Please. Oh, *please.*"

"Sorry, Cassie," said her father. "Our decision is final." He picked up the evening newspaper and settled into his favorite chair.

Cassie's shoulders slumped. She knew the subject was closed.

During the next few days she tried hinting about how nice it would be to have a puppy. All she got were icy stares. At the breakfast table on Saturday morning she decided to give it one last try.

"Mom, Dad, just think how much fun it would be to have a sweet little puppy around the house. They're good for security when they grow up, you know, as watchdogs. And they love you no matter what you do. They never get crabby and they make you feel good and they—"

"*Cassie,* will you drop the subject, *please*?" Her mother gave her a sympathetic smile. "Look, honey, we know how much you want a dog, okay? But we honestly don't think it would be for the best."

Cassie nodded and pretended to pat her mouth with her napkin. She was about to cry, and she didn't want her parents to see her chin quivering.

A little while later she got on her bike and headed for the pet shop again. She had called Suki to see if she wanted to come along. When Mrs. Chen answered the phone, though, she reminded Cassie that Suki had a gym meet.

As she rode through the park, Cassie told herself that she was just going to the pet shop to tell the salesman the bad news. Deep down inside she knew she was hoping that he had actually gone ahead and ordered her a puppy. If he had, maybe she'd be able to take it home on a trial basis. Then she might be able to convince her parents to let her keep it.

"Sorry," said Mr. Willard. "I don't order a pet until I have an order form filled out and a deposit paid. And if the person ordering the pet is a kid, it has to be signed by the kid's parents."

"Oh," Cassie said. She let out a big sigh, and tears came to her eyes. It was no use. She would never get a puppy.

She glanced around at the cages, feeling sadder than ever. The dogs and kittens that had been there were all gone now, and a lonely-looking basset hound sat staring out of its cage at her. It was funny how many cages the store had and so few animals.

She glanced toward the door to the back room. Had Cuda's new owners picked him up? She hoped so. Mr. Willard was definitely not nice to him.

She walked over to the basset's cage and stuck her fingers in. It immediately started licking them.

27

"You're nice, too," said Cassie. "And I bet you'll get a good home real soon."

Suddenly a terrible wail filled the air, making the hair on the back of Cassie's neck stand up. It sounded like a cat. A cat that was in pain.

Cassie looked toward the back door as the cat yowled again. It was the same room where Mr. Willard had taken Cuda. Cassie had an eerie feeling that Cuda had been trying to tell her something. Had he been afraid to go in there?

She glanced at Mr. Willard. He was sitting with his back to her, looking at some papers. How could he not have heard the cat?

She started to call out to him but was cut short by the cat yowling again. It was obviously in pain, and it was also obvious that Mr. Willard wasn't going to do anything about it.

If he doesn't care, I'll find out for myself what's going on, she thought angrily.

She tiptoed over to the door and pressed her ear against it. The cat cries were coming more softly now, but there was misery in the sound.

Cassie slowly turned the knob. She started to push the door open. Suddenly someone grabbed her from behind!

Chapter

Strong hands spun Cassie around.

"That room's private!" shouted Mr. Willard. "Where do you think you're going anyway?" His face had turned beet-red, and his eyes bulged out of their sockets. She could smell his sour breath. He was breathing in fast wheezes.

"I . . . I was looking for a rest room."

"It's back there." He pointed to a door near the fish supplies. He pulled a key out of his pocket. Then he locked the door Cassie had been trying to enter.

Cassie ducked into the rest room and leaned against the wall. "That's it! This is the last time I come here," she muttered to herself. "That man is such a creep!"

She couldn't hear the cat's crying anymore, but

it didn't make her feel any better.

There's definitely something weird about this place, Cassie thought.

In case Mr. Willard was listening, she ran water in the washbasin to make him believe she was washing her hands.

Leaving the rest room, she walked quickly toward the exit. But she suddenly heard a familiar voice and stopped. It was David Ferrante. She ducked behind a display of dog food to listen.

"I accidentally sat on my tarantula," David said. "So I want a new pet."

Cassie clamped a hand over her mouth to keep from bursting out laughing. The thought of David sitting on his revolting spider and squashing it to death was too funny. She buried her face in her hands to muffle the sound of her giggles. But the more Cassie tried to stifle her laughter, the funnier it got.

Then she heard a woman talking.

Peering around the dog food, Cassie saw David kneeling in front of the basset hound's cage. His parents were at the counter with Mr. Willard. She couldn't hear all of what they were saying, just a few words: "dog," "golden retriever," "pet." And it looked as if Mrs. Ferrante was filling out a form. The next thing Cassie knew, David and his parents left the store.

Cassie hesitated a moment to give the Ferrantes time to get in their car and drive away. She didn't want David to know she had been there listening when he confessed to squashing his spider.

When she was sure they had had enough time, she hurried for the door.

Mr. Willard looked up at her. A weird smile spread slowly across his face. He raised his eyebrows and his eyes seemed to sparkle.

Suddenly the room felt hot and stuffy. There was a strange humming sound in her head. She felt dizzy.

Cassie stopped and shook her head, trying to make the sound go away. Her breath was coming in short gasps. "What's going on?" she whispered. "What's happening to me?"

She looked at Mr. Willard. His smile covered his entire face. His watery eyes had turned even blacker.

The heat was sapping Cassie's strength. She turned back to the door. It looked miles away.

"You don't look well, miss," she heard Mr. Willard say. "Here, drink this. It'll make you feel better."

She looked at the glass he was holding out to her. It was filled with a pink liquid.

She hesitated. She was awfully thirsty. Maybe it would help.

Cassie took the glass and swallowed some of the bright-pink liquid. It tasted good—cool and

31

sweet. She gulped down the rest.

"Thanks," she said, and started toward the door again.

Her legs felt as if they were made of lead. It took all her energy to put one foot in front of the other. The hum in Cassie's head grew louder, and the room spun even faster.

One step. Two steps. Cassie stopped and rocked back and forth, trying to keep her balance.

Cassie sank slowly to the floor and closed her eyes. Crackling noises in her ears were drowning out all the other sounds. She felt so tired.

Then everything went black.

Chapter

Cassie felt as if she were trapped in a whirl-pool, struggling to the surface from the depths of a deep black sea. The closer to the surface she got, the brighter it became. The hum in her head slowly faded away.

"It's okay, Cassidy. Everything's fine, girl."

Her eyes fluttered open, and she looked up into Mr. Willard's smiling face. He was reaching toward her. He had something in his beefy hand. *It was a dog collar!*

"Good girl, Cassidy. Good girl," Mr. Willard said in a soothing voice. "You'll be going home soon."

Cassie cringed as Mr. Willard's hand came closer. Trying desperately to back away, she bumped to a stop against something hard. She looked around in a panic. There was nowhere to go! She was in a small metal cage. Mr. Willard fastened the collar around Cassie's neck. Then he slammed the cage door closed and locked it.

"No!" Cassie yelled at him. *"Don't! There's been some mistake!"*

But no words came out. All that came from Cassie's mouth were loud barks.

She tried again. *"Let me out of here! I want to go home!"*

"Shut up your stupid yapping," shouted Mr. Willard.

"Please let me out of here! My parents will be looking for me if I'm not home immediately, and then you'll be in big trouble!"

Mr. Willard's eyes narrowed. He reached through the bars and grabbed the collar, pulling Cassie forward until her nose was mashed against the bars.

She yelped with pain.

"Didn't you hear me?" he said, clenching his teeth and putting his face close to hers. His breath smelled worse than ever. "You'd better shut up, or I'll beat you within an inch of your life."

Cassie looked into his watery black eyes. She knew he meant what he said.

He let go of her collar. With a massive effort he struggled to his feet. He stood glaring down at her.

She didn't dare move. Or make a sound. Her

heart was racing. Cassie had never been so frightened in her life.

She looked down at her arms, and a shudder went through her body. They were completely covered with thick blond fur. She looked at her hands. But all she saw were furry paws! She crossed her eyes and looked down her nose. The tip of it was much too far away—and it was *black*!

Cassie turned and looked behind her. Her body was long and hairy. At the very end of her body Cassie saw—a tail!

Oh, no! she thought. *I'm a—I'm a dog! A half-grown golden retriever. And I'm locked in a cage!* She was a prisoner. Helpless. She couldn't even *talk*.

"One more custom pet, ready for delivery," Mr. Willard said. A sinister smile spread across his fat face. "Oh, what a story you could tell if you could talk, Cassidy." He cackled wildly. "But no one will ever understand your miserable barking."

He threw back his head and laughed hysterically. His huge belly bounced with each chuckle. Mr. Willard was still laughing as he waddled across the store and disappeared into the back room.

Frantically Cassie threw herself against the cage door, trying with all her might to get out. She pawed at the lock, but without fingers she couldn't begin to open it. She bit at it in frustration. That didn't work either. In her desperation she rammed the bars over and over with her shoulders until she was aching and bruised. Finally she sank to the floor in defeat.

She was a dog!

And she was trapped.

Chapter

assie rested her head on her front paws and gazed sadly through the bars.

Were the animals that had been in the cages before custom pets, too? she wondered. She looked at the basset hound. It was lying in the corner of its cage looking back at her.

Cassie opened her mouth, then stopped herself. If she tried to communicate with the basset hound, Mr. Willard would hear. She was scared he'd make good on his threat to beat her if she barked.

If I'm a custom pet, I wonder who ordered me, Cassie thought. *Will it be somebody mean, like Mr. Willard? Will whoever it is be able to understand me and realize that I'm not really a dog?*

Finally, exhausted from trying to escape, Cassie drifted off into a fitful sleep.

A little while later she was startled awake by a noise. She pricked up her ears and shot a quick look in the direction it was coming from.

David Ferrante and his parents were coming in the front door.

"Where is she?" David shouted excitedly. "I want to see her."

Mr. Willard was sitting on his stool again. "Hold your horses, young man. Your parents and I have a little business to take care of first."

"I'm not paying for the dog until I see it and make sure it's what I ordered," boomed Mr. Ferrante.

Mr. Willard shrugged and climbed down from his stool. He motioned for them to follow him and headed straight for Cassie!

Oh, no! she thought with a jolt. *Not David Ferrante's pet! Anything but that!*

She looked around wildly. There was no way to escape. David spotted her and ran to her cage.

"Wow! That was fast. This is her, all right. Exactly the kind of dog I want!" He knelt down and wriggled a hand through the bars.

Cassie backed away, huddling in the corner in terror.

David noticed the nameplate on her cage. He stared at it, and then at her.

"Hey, cool! Her name's Cassidy? I know a girl at school named Cassidy." He chuckled. "And she looks just like you, girl!" he said, pointing a finger in the cage. "She's got a big nose and big feet, too."

"David, what a mean thing to say," his mother scolded.

"Well, it's true," David said defiantly. "She even has the same color hair."

His words hit Cassie like a thunderbolt. *You creep!* she thought angrily. *How dare you say I look like a dog!*

Looking David straight in the eye, Cassie bared her teeth and let out a low growl.

Suddenly Mr. Willard's face appeared in front of the bars. "You'd better not let her get away with growling at you like that," he warned. "She's still young, and she needs plenty of discipline. There's not many things worse than a dog that won't behave."

Cassie could feel the hair standing up all along her spine.

"You don't have to worry about that," Mr. Ferrante assured him. "She'll get plenty of discipline once we get her home. My wife and I were against getting a dog, but David talked us into it. I guarantee you that dog will behave."

Cassie watched as David's father dug out his credit card and followed Mr. Willard to the counter. They were going to pay for her. Buy her just as if she were a sack of groceries.

You can't do that! I'm a girl, not a dog! she wanted to cry out. But she didn't dare make a sound.

Cassie watched as David picked up a leash. She had the feeling that her troubles were just beginning.

Chapter

All the way home Cassie tried to tell the Ferrantes what had happened. But no matter how hard she tried, no one seemed to understand what she was saying.

"I'm not a dog!" Cassie shouted from the backseat. *"I'm a girl! The man in the pet shop gave me something bad to drink, and I passed out. When I woke up I looked like this. Like a dog. Please! Please help me!"* she cried, pacing back and forth across David's lap. He kept trying to hold her down, but each time she struggled free.

"David, will you shut that dog up, for Pete's sake," Mr. Ferrante ordered. "How do you expect me to drive with that yapping in my ear? We're going to have a wreck!"

"Sure, Dad," replied David. He caught Cassie by

41

the collar and pulled a ball out of his pocket. "Good, Cassidy. Settle down, girl. Look. I got you a ball."

He poked the lime-green tennis ball into Cassie's mouth. *He's probably expecting me to chomp down on it so that we can play tug of war,* she thought. *Fat chance!*

The ball was all fuzzy. And it tasted gross! Cassie spat it out and watched it roll under the front seat. *Quadruple yuck. Good riddance.*

David fished it out from under the seat. He held it toward her again. "Come on, girl," he coaxed. "Let's play."

Cassie looked at the ball in disgust. It was covered with spit and had picked up globs of dirt and dried grass from the car floor. There was no way she was going to put that filthy thing in her mouth!

"Here, girl, here. Catch." David pitched the ball into the air. It hit Cassie on the head. Then it bounced off Mrs. Ferrante's shoulder and landed in the front seat.

"David, you know better than to throw a ball in the car," Mrs. Ferrante said.

"Aw, Mom," said David. "I was just playing with Cassidy so she wouldn't bark."

"Well, keep the ball in the backseat," she warned. She glared at Cassie as if to warn her, too.

Cassie was glad when the car finally pulled to a

stop in the Ferrantes' driveway a few minutes later.

Maybe when they open the car door, I can make a break for it, she thought.

But her hopes were dashed immediately. The instant her feet hit the ground, David grabbed her leash and began dragging her toward the house. The tightness of the collar made her stick her tongue out. She had to trot to keep up as he raced through the house to the kitchen.

"Are you hungry, Cassidy?" he asked. "How about some water? Mom and Dad say if I'm going to have a dog, I have to take care of it. I'm going to take the best care of you in the world."

While he was talking to her, he was filling two big plastic bowls. One had water in it, and the other had revolting-looking dry dog food. Then he set the bowls on the floor and stood back, beaming proudly.

"There you are, girl. Go ahead. Have some."

Cassie looked first at David and then at the bowls.

"But they're on the floor! You can't expect me to eat on the floor!" she shouted.

David swooped down and clamped Cassie's mouth shut with both hands. He squeezed so hard, tears of pain spurted into her eyes.

His eyes were wide with concern. "Shhhhh! No

43

more barking," he said. "Don't you understand? My parents don't even like dogs. You'd better watch it, or we'll both be in trouble."

Cassie wriggled out of his grasp and headed for the living room. She had never been more frustrated in her life. All she wanted was to get away by herself and bawl her eyes out in peace. She looked first one way and then the other to be sure the coast was clear. Then she jumped up on the sofa and curled up in a ball. If she pretended to be asleep, David might leave her alone.

"Get that dog off the furniture!"

Startled at the sound, she looked up to see Mrs. Ferrante standing in the doorway. David came barreling into the room and grabbed Cassie by the collar and hauled her off the couch.

"Bad dog!" he yelled. "Bad Cassidy!"

This is so humiliating, Cassie thought. *I hate being a dog!* She didn't want to eat on the floor. And she didn't want to sit on it either. It was hard, and the scratchy living-room carpet was making her itch all over.

"Won't anybody listen!" she wailed. *"I'm not a dog! I'm a girl!"*

Just then Mr. Ferrante charged into the room. His fists were clenched. His face was a beet-red.

Cassie lowered her head and tucked her tail be-

44

tween her legs. Mr. Ferrante was headed straight for her.

"Let me at that dog!" he cried. "*I'll* make her shut up for good!"

Chapter

"Wait, Dad! Don't hurt her," David pleaded. He jumped in front of Cassie and put his arms around her protectively. "I was just going to take Cassidy for a walk."

For the first time since she had known him, Cassie actually appreciated David. For an instant she almost liked him.

"You'd better get her out of my sight fast if you don't want to see me teach her a lesson she won't forget," snarled Mr. Ferrante. "I'll never understand why we let you talk us into buying a dog." He frowned as he watched David fasten the leash to Cassie's collar and lead her out the door.

She followed David at a run, afraid even to look back. As soon as they were outside, she looked up at David and wagged her tail. She started to say thanks but remembered that it would just come out a bark.

"Let's go to the park," David said, patting her on the head. "I want to show you to my friends."

Cassie's heart leaped. She knew all those kids. Maybe she could make one of them understand her.

But as she trotted along at David's heel, her optimism gave way to other problems. The pavement was so hot that it burned the soft pads on the bottom of her feet. Pesky bugs whizzed around her nose and dug into her coat, making her neck itch so badly that she had to stop. She tried to reach a front paw up to scratch, but her leg wouldn't bend in that direction. Then she remembered she didn't have fingers, just short furry toes! Frustrated, she sat down on the hot sidewalk and scratched her neck with a back leg.

Yuuuck! she thought. *Fleas!*

They came to a street crossing where the traffic light was red. As they waited for it to change, Cassie peered fearfully from behind David's legs at the cars zooming by. They loomed like huge monsters, belching foul-smelling exhaust fumes, their horns blaring. They were terrifying!

She was trembling and her tail was tucked between her legs when the light finally turned green. She didn't want to go into the street.

What if she got run over? It happened to dogs all the time.

"Come on, Cassidy," David urged, tugging on her leash. "It's okay."

She stepped gingerly off the curb, casting a fearful glance at the cars. Their engines growled like tigers about to spring. The smell of exhaust stung her nose. What if one of the cars shot ahead? She'd be killed!

Traffic was never this scary when I was a girl, she thought.

David yanked on her leash. Cassie pulled back, but he dragged her away from the curb and out into the intersection.

Cassie looked up at the grilles of the cars waiting to come at her. There was no turning back. She leaped forward, almost jerking David off his feet, and ran for the opposite curb.

"Geez, Cassidy," said David, rubbing the hand that had been holding the leash. "You just about tore my hand off."

Safely on the other side, they strolled along a residential street that was shaded by giant trees. Cassie relaxed a little and thought about what she would do when they got to the park. It was obvious that barking wouldn't do any good. She had found that out the hard way.

Maybe I can do some kind of trick, she

49

thought. *Something that dogs don't usually do. But what?*

She was trotting along, trying to think of a good trick, when she glanced up the sidewalk. Coming straight toward her and David was a grouchy-looking man leading a huge black rottweiler.

The dog was wearing a spiked collar. He bared his fangs and began growling when he spotted Cassidy.

Uh-oh, Cassie thought, feeling suddenly panicky. *I must be in his territory or something. Whatever it is, he definitely doesn't like me!*

Suddenly the dog lunged and broke loose. Snarling furiously, he raced for Cassidy!

Chapter

12

assie stared in horror at the charging dog. He had a bloodthirsty look in his eyes. His jaws were open wide, showing long white fangs. Saliva drooled from his mouth. She froze with fright. Her heart pounded as he came bounding toward her. She could almost feel his teeth ripping into her throat.

David yelled and pulled frantically on her leash. But the rottweiler was almost on them. There was no escape.

Cassie crouched low and scrunched her eyes shut, waiting for him to slam into her.

Nothing happened.

Opening one eye, she peeked out. The huge black dog had stopped in his tracks just inches from her. He was looking down at her, twisting his head first one way and then another.

With a little whimper he lay down in front of her and rested his nose on his paws. Their noses were almost touching. His eyes were soft and pleading.

Cassie raised her head and blinked in surprise. Her heart began to slow down. She didn't know what had made the rottweiler stop; she was just thankful to be alive.

Cassie looked at the huge black dog more closely. Had she seen him before? Yes! In Custom Pets.

It was Cuda!

"What's the big idea of letting your big old vicious dog attack my little Cassidy!" demanded David. "She's just a pup. He could have killed her!"

The man knitted his eyebrows together angrily and shook his fist at David. "Don't raise your voice at me, you young hoodlum. I've seen you around before. You're nothing but a troublemaker."

Neither of them seemed to notice that Cassidy and Cuda weren't fighting.

"Oh, yeah? Well, you'll have plenty of trouble if your dog hurts my dog," countered David.

Cassie felt a rush of excitement. Cuda seemed to recognize her. *If only I can communicate with him,* she thought.

While David and the man continued yelling at each other, Cassie stood up and bent over Cuda.

"*Cuda? Is that really you?*" she asked.

Cuda jumped to his feet and began wagging his nub of a tail furiously. His mouth was open in what resembled a big grin. His eyes sparkled at her brightly.

Cassidy wagged back. *He understands,* she thought happily.

"*I'm so glad to see you,*" she said.

Cuda touched his nose to the tip of hers. She had seen dogs do this before. It was how they made friends.

If he barks back, will I know what he's trying to say? Or will it only sound like barking to me? she wondered. *I sure hope not. I have so many questions to ask him.*

"*I'm scared,*" Cassie said. "*I don't understand what happened to us. Do you? Is there any way we can get back to our human bodies?*"

Cuda's eyes lit up, as if he knew exactly what she was saying.

Just then the grouchy man grabbed Cuda's leash. "Come on, Cuda. Let's get out of here and finish your walk," he grumbled, jerking the dog away. "I've had enough of this rude boy and his yapping dog."

Cuda looked alarmed. He tried to resist, but the man was too strong and dragged him along the sidewalk.

"*Cuda, say something!*" cried Cassie.

53

Cuda opened his mouth to bark, but before anything could come out, the man jerked on his leash again, choking off the sound.

"David, come on! Let's go after them!" Cassie insisted. She tugged on her own leash and leaned in the direction Cuda was being taken. *"I have to talk to Cuda."*

"Easy, Cassidy. Easy, girl. Don't be afraid. He won't hurt you now," David said. "I made sure of that."

Cassie jumped up, putting her front paws on David's chest. She looked him straight in the eye. *"No! No! You don't understand!"*

David pushed her down. "Don't bark in my face, you stupid dog," he said in a disgusted voice.

Cassie was frantic as she watched the man lead Cuda around the corner and out of sight.

What will I do now? she thought desperately. *Cuda is the only one who understands me. He might know what happened to us. What if I never see him again?*

Chapter

"Come on, girl," said David, heading down the street. "Let's go to the park."

Cassie took one last look as Cuda and his master disappeared around a corner. Her heart sank. There was nothing else she could do. She trotted after David.

By the time they reached the park, she was miserable. She was hot from running in a fur coat in the blazing summer sunshine. Bugs were dive-bombing her face, getting in her eyes and flying up her nose. She was so thirsty that her tongue was hanging out the side of her mouth, almost dragging on the ground.

David must have noticed, because he tugged on her leash and said, "Hey, Cassidy. Here's a puddle. Get a drink."

Cassie's eyes widened in horror. A puddle! He didn't really expect her to drink filthy, muddy water that people had walked through!

"Get serious!" she cried. *"There's got to be a drinking fountain around here somewhere."*

"Barking's just going to make you thirstier," said David, shaking his head and frowning. "I don't know about you, Cassidy. You don't act very smart."

She made a low growl rumble in the back of her throat. She was getting tired of David again.

"Are you going to get a drink, or aren't you?" David asked impatiently. "I haven't got all day, you know."

Cassie lowered her head, slinking toward the puddle. *What if I get sick?* she thought as she stared down into the brown water. She lowered the tip of her tongue into it. At least it felt cool. Closing her eyes, she lapped up a mouthful and gulped it down quickly.

Quadruple yuck!

It tasted awful! And it left a layer of grit all over her tongue.

"Come on, Cassidy, let's go," David urged. "I think I hear some of the guys at the baseball diamond."

Cassidy trudged after him, hoping there would be some shade near the diamond where she could

56

stretch out on her stomach and cool off.

"Hey, look, everybody! Ferrante's got a dog!" Ken shouted the instant they came in sight of the ball field.

"Hey, yeah! Look!" yelled Todd. "He's neat. Where'd you get him?"

"Here, boy. Here, boy," called Max.

"She's not a boy, she's a girl," David corrected him. "I got her at the same pet shop where I got Igor."

"You mean the custom pet shop?" asked Todd. "Cool! Did you order her, too?"

David nodded as the boys all crowded around Cassie.

"Wow! She's a beauty. What's her name?" asked Max, kneeling down and gently stroking her head.

David burst out laughing. "You're not going to believe this, but she already had a name when I got her. It's Cassidy. You know, like Cassidy Cavanaugh in our class at school."

"Yeah, I can even see the resemblance," said Ken, chuckling.

"Me, too," said Todd, making a silly face at Cassie.

All the boys were laughing now, and Cassie wished that she could hide somewhere. Even more than that, she wanted desperately to get off the leash and run for home. "Here, Cassidy. Here, girl. Fetch!" yelled Todd.

Cassie looked up to see a stick flying past her nose and soaring into the air. She watched as it arched upward, hanging there for an instant, and then plummeted to the earth.

"She's not very smart, is she?" asked Todd.

"Hey, you stupid dog, don't you even know what 'fetch' means?" cried David.

"She's not full-grown yet," said Max. "Maybe she hasn't been taught how to fetch."

Cassie cast a grateful look in Max's direction. *He's the only intelligent one here,* she thought.

"I've got an idea," said Todd. "You show her how it's done, David. I'll throw the stick again, and you run over and pick it up in your mouth and bring it to me."

Todd broke up laughing at his own joke, and Ken and Max did, too.

David wasn't laughing. His face had turned bright red and was filled with rage.

"That's not funny," he said. "She'll learn how to fetch—right now!" He picked up a stick and stomped toward Cassie.

Cassie tucked her tail and looked up at him in terror. Even though he had been extra nice to her when his parents got angry, she had seen David do mean things before. She wasn't sure what to expect.

David waggled the stick under her nose. "You see this? It's a stick!" he said in a commanding voice. "You got that? It's a *stick!*"

Cassie looked at the stick and then back at David.

"I'm going to throw it, see. And you'd better go get it and bring it back to me if you know what's good for you."

I know I ought to do what David says, thought Cassie, *but I just can't fetch a dumb old stick. It's humiliating. I'm a girl, not a dog!*

David raised his arm and let the stick fly. "Go get it, girl. Show them how smart you are."

Cassie planted her bottom firmly on the grass.

"Cassidy!" shrieked David. "I said fetch!"

Her heart was pounding, but she didn't move.

Suddenly David went into a rage. "I told you to fetch, you dumb mutt!" He raced toward her, stopping and pulling back his foot to kick her.

Cassie closed her eyes, waiting for the blow.

"Stop! Don't you kick that dog, David Ferrante! You'll hurt her!"

Cassie couldn't believe her ears. It was Suki! And she was riding her bike up the path straight toward them. *She'll help me!* Cassie thought with a rush of hope. *She'll know it's me!*

"Look out. Here comes Suki-Pukey," Ken said sarcastically. "Oh, boy, am I scared."

"Me, too," said Todd, giggling. "She's probably mad enough to puke all over us."

Cassie broke loose and took off at a run for Suki. *"Suki! Suki! It's me, Cassie!"* she shouted. *"You've got to help me! The man at the pet store turned me into a dog!"*

Suki's expression changed to shock and then horror as Cassie sprinted toward her. Her mouth fell open, and her eyes widened with fright. Suki tried to jerk her bike around but lost her balance and tumbled to the ground, getting her feet tangled.

"David, call off your dog!" she screamed.

Cassie was standing over her now. *"No, Suki. It's me!"* she cried. *"You've got to help me! Please!"*

"Get her away from me! She's going to bite!" Suki cried hysterically. She scooted away from Cassie.

Cassie could hear David and the others running toward her, shouting at her. But suddenly it didn't matter. It didn't even matter if David kicked her or Mr. Ferrante beat her when they got home.

Suki Chen had been her best friend forever, and even *she* didn't recognize Cassie.

Even worse, Suki was afraid of her!

Cassie felt her heart breaking into little pieces.

Chapter

14

For the next few days Cassie was so busy sur-viving, she didn't have time to think about Suki or Cuda. She was having enough trouble adjusting to her life as a dog.

For one thing, there was the food. She had re-fused to touch the dry dog food in the bowl on the floor. One sniff had told Cassie that it would taste unbelievably gross. To make things worse, Mrs. Ferrante cooked the most delicious-smelling meals in the world.

The first night Cassie was there, Mrs. Ferrante made fried chicken. And mashed potatoes and gravy. And apple pie. When Cassie smelled them, she thought she would die.

She had lain on the living-room floor, with her nose resting on her front paws just inside the kitchen. Her mouth watered as she took in the delicious aromas. She had sent pleading look after pleading look in David's direction, but he hadn't noticed. She hadn't been given a single bite.

The second night David's mother fixed potato salad while Mr. Ferrante cooked hamburgers outside on the grill. This time Cassie managed to get her whole body into the kitchen and whimpered softly. Still David didn't notice or toss her even the tiniest morsel.

By the third night she was desperate. It got even worse when David answered the front door and a delivery boy handed him two huge pizza boxes. She trotted behind David, sniffing the air, as he carried them into the kitchen.

"Which would you rather have, David, sausage or pepperoni?" asked his mother when the Ferrantes were seated. The spicy aroma filled the air, making Cassie's mouth water furiously.

She managed to sneak all the way into the dining area and under the table while the family's attention was on the pizza. Putting her chin on David's leg, she looked up at him with the saddest eyes she could make.

David couldn't help noticing her. He darted quick looks at his parents and slowly lowered the pizza wedge back to his plate. Quickly ripping off a piece, he jabbed it into Cassie's mouth and went on eating as if nothing were going on under the table.

Cassie almost died of happiness. The flavor was heavenly. Thick, creamy cheese, tangy tomato sauce, and spicy pepperoni.

"More," she whimpered softly. *"Please, David, another piece."*

David gave her another. This time it was just a flavorless half-moon of crust. *Oh, well,* she thought. *At least it's better than dog food.*

She had eaten four bites of pizza and two crusts when David's father accidentally dropped his napkin on the floor. Bending over to retrieve it, he came eye to eye and nose to nose with Cassie.

"Da-*vid!*" he roared, exploding upward and bumping his head on the table. "Are you feeding that dog off the *table?*" he said, rubbing his head.

David turned pale. "I . . . I just gave her a little bit," he fumbled.

Underneath the table Cassie trembled in fear.

"David, wash your hands immediately," ordered his mother. "That dog has probably licked your fingers."

David scooted his chair out and left the table.

"I'm warning you for the last time, David, that

dog has got to learn some manners," shouted his father.

At the same instant, Mr. Ferrante grabbed Cassie by the collar. Dragging her out from under the table, he zoomed across the room, pulling her with him.

"When you're hungry, you eat this," he ordered. He pushed her nose painfully into the hard pellets of food in her food bowl.

"And, David, if you want to keep this dog, you'd better make sure she stays away from the table at mealtime. And that's final!"

Cassie started to yell at them again and tell them for the millionth time that she was a girl, not a dog. But she didn't.

Get real, she told herself. *They can't understand me. And as far as they're concerned, I am a dog!*

Reluctantly she began eating the food in her dish. She was desperately hungry, and she had to eat something. Even if it was out of a bowl on the floor.

The dry dog food tasted like cardboard. It tasted like sawdust. It tasted like ground-up rocks. Cassie looked over at the bag. It had a picture of a rare piece of steak on it. The words "Your Dog Will Love Puppy Bits!" were printed in yellow letters.

Right, Cassie thought. *I really love this junk.*

The dry food stuck in Cassie's throat, but she kept eating. Unless she wanted to starve to death, it was all she could do.

Chapter

15

"In my day a dog was a *dog,*" Mr. Ferrante said one evening at the dinner table.

Cassie was lounging on the living-room floor enjoying the mouthwatering aroma of lasagna wafting in from the kitchen. His words rudely interrupted her thoughts of the fabulous bites she knew David was squirreling away for her in his napkin.

She raised her head and frowned at Mr. Ferrante through the open doorway. *Uh-oh,* she thought. *I don't like the sound of this.*

"Yes, siree, when I was a boy, the old saying 'man's best friend' really meant something," he went on. "None of this business of a dog lying around in the air-conditioning getting fat and lazy. *My* dog was a crackerjack of a hunting dog. That's why I named

67

him Cracker Jack," he said proudly. "Old Cracker Jack slept in the barn and never set foot in the house."

"Yeah, but Cassidy's a house dog," said David.

"What do you mean, Cassidy's a house dog?" Mr. Ferrante asked in amazement. "She's a golden retriever, isn't she? How do you think the breed got its name?"

"Because they're good hunting dogs," replied David, sounding bored with the whole idea. "Not Cassidy, though. I tried to teach her to fetch a stick at the park the other day. She was too dumb to catch on."

David's words stung Cassie.

I am not dumb! What's dumb is fetching a stupid stick. And I'm not fat and lazy, either!

"Honey, you know you could use a day off from work," David's mother said to her husband. "Why don't you and David take Cassidy out to Uncle Charlie's farm tomorrow and teach her to hunt. I'll pack you a big lunch to take along. It might help you and Cassidy get better acquainted and learn to like each other. All three of you would enjoy it."

Cassie groaned silently. *Fat chance of Mr. Grouchy and me getting along!* she thought.

"That's not a bad idea," Mr. Ferrante said, his

voice rising in anticipation. "How about it, David?"

"I guess so," David answered.

Cassie crawled under a chair in the living room and listened with dread to David's father making plans.

The next morning came too soon for Cassie. It was dark when Mr. Ferrante loaded the back of the family car with duck decoys, their lunches, and two gun-carrying cases. She hadn't seen him so happy. She, on the other hand, was miserable at the thought of wading in water to retrieve cold, dead birds.

When they arrived at Uncle Charlie's farm, Mr. Ferrante stuck shotgun shells in the holders on his khaki hunting jacket. Then he took a monstrous-looking shotgun out of one carrying case and a smaller one out of the other. He gave the small gun to David.

Shifting his red hunting cap on his head, he slapped David on the back good-naturedly. "This was a great idea, son. Are we gonna have fun today, or what?"

Next he stuck two fingers in his mouth and gave a shrill whistle. "Head 'em up, and move 'em out," he commanded cheerfully.

Cassie lay down in the grass and watched as father and son started off down an old wagon track.

69

They hadn't gone far before they realized she wasn't with them and turned around.

"Cassidy! Here, girl," Mr. Ferrante called.

She didn't budge.

"Come on, Cassidy," David called. "It's going to be fun."

Cassidy ignored them, scratching a flea bite near her tail instead.

Mr. Ferrante hurried back to where she was lying. He grabbed her by the collar and gave it a sharp jerk. "Get moving, Cassidy. It's time you earned your keep."

Cassie trailed along reluctantly, her tail down. Before long she realized—even though she would never have admitted it to the Ferrantes—she was beginning to enjoy the fresh morning air. The sun had come up and was burning the dew off the grass. The air was crisp.

Just as she was beginning to forget why they had come, there was a loud whir of wings, and four birds flew up right under her nose. Cassie tangled her feet and fell over herself trying to jump out of the way.

"Fire just in front of them!" commanded Mr. Ferrante.

Two thunderous BOOMS! went off behind Cassie. She leaped forward and almost collapsed out of fear.

"Go get 'em, Cassidy!" yelled Mr. Ferrante.

She looked back at him in amazement. Her heart was pounding so hard, she thought it would jump right out of her body. But she didn't move.

"Didn't you hear me, Cassidy? Fetch!" he cried, waving the barrel of his gun first in the direction of the fallen birds and then toward her.

She trembled as she stared down the gun barrel. Was he pointing it toward her on purpose? she wondered. Would he actually shoot her if she didn't go get the birds?

She decided not to wait around to find out.

Her ears still ringing from the blasts, Cassie ran across the field to the edge of a small lake where she had seen one of the birds go down. It was lying crumpled in the shallow water, its neck twisted back. Its beautiful feathers were in disarray. It looked disgusting.

She circled it. Did he honestly expect her to pick it up? *In her mouth?*

Cassie looked back at Mr. Ferrante. His gun was still pointed toward her.

She cautiously stuck one paw into the water. It was cold. She glanced back at Mr. Ferrante and David again. They were still watching her.

Slowly Cassie eased herself into the muddy water and nuzzled the dead bird with her nose. It was soft.

71

Eeee . . . YUUCK! It was still warm! *Quadruple yuck!* she thought.

She looked back over her shoulder again. Mr. Ferrante was watching every move she made.

Turning back to the bird, she gingerly took it in her teeth by the tip of one wing. She almost gagged a hundred times as she carried it, dangling from her mouth, back across the field. She dropped it twenty feet away from David and his father.

"Don't put it down there, bring it here, you dumb dog," called Mr. Ferrante.

Cassie turned her back on him, refusing to listen. She had had enough! What's more, she wasn't about to be a part of killing poor animals just for sport. After all, she was an animal herself now, too!

"I don't think Cassidy likes hunting," David said. "Can't we go home now?"

"Of course not," huffed his father. "We're here to have *fun*."

Mr. Ferrante got angrier and angrier each time he shot a bird and Cassie refused to go after it. He didn't seem to notice that David had stopped shooting. Finally he loaded everything back into the car.

It was a very quiet trip home.

That night Cassie had to sleep in the basement.

The next evening Cassie was resting on the floor beside the sofa when the local news came on television. She had never been much of a news fan, but her ears pricked up when she heard the announcer say, "Local police have joined in the search for a missing twelve-year-old girl. Cassidy Cavanaugh, known to her friends as Cassie, has not been seen since Saturday morning, when she left home to go shopping."

Cassie jumped to her feet and ran to the set. *"Look!"* she shouted. *"That's me they're talking about! That's my picture they're showing on TV!"*

Mr. Ferrante slammed his hand down on the table beside his chair. "Shut that dog up, David," he roared. "I can't hear a thing they're saying."

"Hush, Cassidy," said David. His eyes were on the set. "A girl from my school is missing. Her name's Cassidy, just like yours. She's in my class."

"Of course she is, you jerk," Cassie shouted, running in circles around the room. *"I'm Cassidy. Look at me. Remember how you said I looked like the Cassidy in your class? Long nose. Blond hair. David, it's me!"*

Running to the television set again, she rose up on her back legs, pawing desperately at the screen. *"Here I am!"* she cried in frustration. *"I belong to David Ferrante, and I'm a dog! Why can't anyone understand me?"*

"Didn't you hear me? I said shut up!" David warned. He pulled her away from the set and grabbed her nose, squeezing it shut so that she couldn't bark. "If you don't be quiet, I'm going to have to get you a muzzle."

Tears of pain squirted out of Cassie's eyes. Her pride hurt even worse. *How dare David squeeze my nose!* she thought indignantly. *I was only trying to tell him something. Something important!*

Cassie lay awake all night at the foot of David's bed. She had to find some way to make him pay attention to her. To understand. Barking certainly wouldn't do it. She had found that out the hard way.

There must be something else I can do to get his attention, she thought. *But what?*

It was almost morning when an idea came to her. She would get his attention, all right. She was so angry and so frustrated that it didn't matter what happened. She would get it good.

She waited until the house was empty. David was playing at a friend's house. His father had gone to work, and his mother was grocery shopping. The timing was perfect.

Cassie started in David's closet. She dug through the mound of dirty clothes, the empty potato-chip bags, the catcher's mitt and soccer ball, until she found what she was looking for.

David's prize basketball sneakers!

She dragged one of them out into the middle of his bedroom floor and growled at it as if it were her biggest enemy.

Just wait until he sees this, she thought, her eyes gleaming and her fangs bared.

Cassie lunged at the shoe, grabbing it in her teeth and snarling as she shook it and wrestled it around the floor. The next instant she dropped it.

Pee-YEW! she cried. *It stinks!*

She sat back on her haunches and looked at the sneaker. She didn't know if she could bring herself to do what needed to be done. It was just too smelly.

75

Holding her breath, Cassie grabbed the shoe again. Her sharp teeth punctured the soft leather. Next she held it tightly with her front paws, tearing and tearing at the tongue until it was in shreds.

This is starting to be fun, she thought gleefully. *Now for the serious part!*

She plunged her nose into the shoe, jerking out the inner lining and spitting it out an instant later.

Wow! It tasted ten times worse than it smelled!

As soon as she had finished destroying the sneaker, Cassie barreled into the table beside David's bed, sending his model-airplane collection all over he floor. Then she rolled on every one of them, smashing them into a million slivers of wood.

Next she pulled the covers off his bed, ripping open his pillow and watching as a cloud of white feathers burst into the air and settled over everything like a gentle snowfall.

There! If that doesn't get his attention, nothing will, she thought, surveying the destruction with satisfaction. *Now maybe he'll try to understand me!*

Curling up in a ball in the middle of the disheveled mound of sheets and blankets, Cassie fell into an exhausted sleep.

"**O**bedience school!" David's father thundered when he got home from work and heard about Cassidy's latest escapade.

Cassie was hiding under David's bed. When she heard his enraged voice, she scooted deeper, burying herself among the dirty socks and forgotten toys that littered the floor.

Her plan had backfired. David hadn't gotten the message. He had scolded her for messing up his things. To make things even worse, now she had to go to *obedience school*.

"You'll go with her, David, and learn how to control her," Mr. Ferrante continued, "and you'll start tomorrow."

Cassie shivered nervously as Mrs. Ferrante dropped her and David off the next day at obedience school. Before they left home, David had replaced her leather collar with a choke-chain training collar that could be jerked painfully if she disobeyed. She shook her head back and forth, trying to adjust to the weight of the chain.

The classes were being held in the park across the street from Custom Pets. Cassie looked fearfully at the vine-covered building, wondering if Mr. Willard was watching.

But she didn't have much time to worry about it. A dozen or so dogs and their owners were already crowded around the instructor. David led her over to the group.

Cassie looked up at the instructor. Her heart skipped a beat. He was a big, burly man with a crooked nose and massive arms. His mouth seemed to be turned downward in a permanent frown. He reminded her more of a lion tamer than a dog trainer.

David must have noticed how mean he looked, too. He leaned down to Cassie and said, "He looks like he wrestles alligators for a living. You'd better do everything he tells you, girl."

The instructor held up a hand. "Okay, everybody. Time to get started. My name's Bruiser, and I'm going to teach you how to control your dogs."

Bruiser! Cassie thought with alarm. He obviously had gotten the name for a good reason.

"Everybody line up in front of me with your dogs," he ordered. "The first thing we're going to learn is sit and stay. And remember, *absolutely no barking.*"

Cassie trotted meekly along at David's side as they joined the line that was forming in front of Bruiser. If she could have crossed her toes for luck, she would have. Instead she promised herself that she would do exactly as she was told. She certainly didn't want to attract the wrath of Bruiser or make David yank on the choke collar. He had demonstrated at home how it would tighten up and choke her when he pulled on her leash.

As soon as they were in line, Cassie glanced around at the other dogs. There were two poodles, a miniature schnauzer, another golden retriever, and—

Her heart leaped with joy. At the end of the line was a grouchy-looking man and a black rottweiler wearing a spiked collar. It was Cuda!

Instantly Cassie forgot all about Bruiser. *"Cuda!"* she called out joyfully. *"It's me, Cassie. Remember? From the pet—"*

A sharp pain in her throat cut off her words.

"Shut up, Cassidy," David whispered loudly. "Bruiser said no barking."

Bruiser was glaring at them. "Control your dog, young man."

"Yes, sir," David said meekly. He was holding the choke chain so tight, Cassie could barely breath. It was so tight, her tongue was hanging out of her mouth.

Cassie obeyed Bruiser completely and sat and stayed four times before she dared look down the line at Cuda again. He was looking back! Giving her a big doggie smile!

In spite of the warnings she jumped to her feet, wagging her tail furiously and pulling on the leash.

"Cuda! Say something to me. I need to talk to you!"

A sudden pain in her throat reminded her of her mistake. But this time it wasn't David pulling on her leash.

Bruiser had grabbed it and was jerking furiously. "Sit!" he commanded, shoving her rear end down and pulling up hard on her collar.

Cassie was filled with panic. It hurt. What was he doing? Why wouldn't he let go!

The pain made lights explode before her eyes like fireworks. She couldn't breathe and her lungs screamed for air.

She had to make him stop. She had to get away.

Frantically she lunged, sinking her teeth into his arm. An instant later she felt a sharp crack on the head.

Everything went black.

Chapter

"**E**xpelled! What do you mean, Cassidy was *expelled* from obedience school?" Mr. Ferrante asked between clenched teeth. His face was purple with rage. Cassie wouldn't have been surprised to see fire and smoke pouring out his nose.

But for once she couldn't care less that David's father was furious. Her head throbbed so badly, it made her eyes cross. And a lump the size of an egg was rising behind her left ear.

Mr. Ferrante threw up his hands after he heard David's explanation of what happened. "Bit the instructor! What will that dog do next?"

"But, Dad, it wasn't Cassidy's fault. Bruiser was being mean," David said. "He really hurt her."

His father began pacing the floor. He glared

first at Cassie and then at David.

"Suppose the man sues. What will we do then?"

"Maybe if you just pay for his stitches," David offered.

"So now he's got stitches!" cried Mr. Ferrante. "And I suppose he'll have to take a tetanus shot and be tested for rabies. Do we get to pay for that, too? No way. I've had it. This dog goes back to the pet store right now, and we're demanding our money back."

Cassidy's ears pricked up, and she forgot all about her headache. The thought of returning to Custom Pets terrified her. There was no telling what evil things Mr. Willard had in the back room or what he might do to her if the Ferrantes brought her back and asked for a refund.

"Please, Dad," cried David. He dropped to his knees beside Cassie and put his arms around her. "Don't make me take Cassidy back to the pet shop. *Please!* She's the only dog I've ever had, and I *love* her." He buried his face in her fur and nuzzled her. Looking up into David's face, Cassie saw his eyes were brimming with tears. To her surprise she felt an unexpected rush of affection for him. *Maybe he isn't a total jerk, after all,* she thought. She gave his cheek a big slurpy kiss.

What's the matter with me? she thought with a jolt. *I just kissed David Ferrante! I would never do a thing like that in a million years. Besides, I don't want to be his dog forever. I want to go back to being a girl!*

"I think you'd better take Cassidy out in the backyard for a little while, David, and let your father and me discuss the situation," suggested Mrs. Ferrante.

"Okay," David said. "Come on, Cassidy. Let's go out and play."

David picked up his basketball and made shots while Cassie stretched out under a shade tree. Every once in a while she glanced nervously at the back door of the house. David's parents were in there deciding her fate, and there wasn't a single thing she could do about it!

After a while, when they still hadn't come out, she shifted her attention to a dripping water faucet that was making a big mud puddle beside the back door. Drip. Drip. Drip. The hypnotic dripping made her feel sleepy. Drip. Drip. Drip. Her eyelids started to droop.

Suddenly they popped open again. She looked closer at the puddle. Paw prints! She had made them when she and David came outside.

Cassie jumped to her feet and ran to the mud. *I've finally found it!* she thought gleefully. *A way to make them understand!*

She glanced around the yard. David had stopped shooting baskets and was building a model airplane on the picnic table. *Good,* she thought. *He won't notice what I'm doing until I'm finished.*

She stood back, looking over the soft, damp earth like an artist studying her canvas. Then she started to work.

She pawed at the mud for a long time, working hard to get it just right. Her front toes didn't move as easily as fingers, and she had to smooth over what she was doing and start again. Her frustration almost caused her to give up, but the thought of Mr. Willard and Custom Pets made her keep going.

When she was finished, she stood back and proudly looked over what she had done. With the jab of a paw, she put a dot over the letter *i.*

She grinned. Written in the soft, dark mud were the words:

HELP! NOT DOG! GIRL!

Chapter

19

assie watched the back door expectantly. David's parents had been inside an awfully long time. One of them had to come out soon.

Time dragged on. Even David was beginning to fidget and toss worried glances at the door.

Cassie looked again at the words she had written in the mud:

HELP! NOT DOG! GIRL!

Pretty impressive, if you ask me, she thought proudly.

Finally the back door opened, and Mrs. Ferrante stepped out onto the porch.

Cassie shot to attention.

"Time to come in for supper, David," she called.

"But, Mom. What about Cassidy?" David asked. "Did you and Dad make up your minds? Can I keep her? Please?"

Cassie pricked up her ears.

"We'll talk about it at dinner, dear," she replied. Her voice gave no clue as to what had been decided. "Hurry in now, and don't forget to wash your hands."

She turned to go back inside without so much as a glance in Cassie's direction or at the mud where Cassie had written the message.

Cassie jumped up. *"Hey, look over here! I wrote you a message! You've got to read it! Please!"*

"Doesn't that dog know how to do anything but bark?" Mrs. Ferrante asked with disgust.

Galloping over to the back porch, Cassie stood up on her back legs in front of Mrs. Ferrante and pawed at the air. *"Come on,"* she insisted. *"Follow me. I've got something to show you!"*

When Mrs. Ferrante didn't make a move to follow her, Cassie ran to David, jumping on him and almost knocking him down.

"Don't let her go in! Make her look at the mud. If you come, maybe she'll follow!" she cried. Cassie grabbed his pant leg in her teeth and pulled him toward the mud.

"Cut it out, Cassidy," cried David. He swatted at her and tried to pull his pant leg out of her mouth. "The more you bark, the more Mom and Dad are likely to send you back to the pet store. Don't you know anything, you stupid dog?"

Cassie held on tight and pulled him toward the mud.

David shrugged at his mother. "I think there's something Cassidy wants to show us."

"What on earth?" grumbled Mrs. Ferrante, frowning. She came down the porch steps.

She was coming, too! It was only a matter of minutes—seconds maybe—until the truth would come out. Surely they would want to help her. Together they could find a way to turn her back into a girl again.

Cassie trotted over to her message. *"See?"* she asked, running in circles. *"Do you understand now?"*

Mrs. Ferrante stopped and stared at Cassie in surprise.

Suddenly Cassie was dizzy with hope. Had David's mother read the message already? Even a split second of waiting seemed like an hour.

"Look at that dog!" cried Mrs. Ferrante. "She's covered with mud! It's all over her paws and in her coat. Even her nose is muddy! I'll not allow her to step one foot into my clean house.

She'll have to sleep in the yard tonight!"

With that Mrs. Ferrante spun around and marched to the house, dragging David along by the arm.

Cassie watched in disbelief. She lowered her head and tail. *It's no use, she thought. I'll never make them understand. I'll be a dog forever.*

Chapter

C assie spent the night curled up under a bush in the backyard. She scratched her fleas and worried. She was scared. What if they decided to send her back to Custom Pets? She pictured Mr. Willard's black watery eyes staring at her, his cold smile just before he gave her the pink liquid to drink.

Cassie remembered the painful wail of the cat. What cruel things was he doing to animals in the back room?

David had come out once before dark to pat her head and mumble that she'd better be awfully good. He'd had a pretty tough time talking his parents into giving her *one last chance*.

Cassie felt so helpless.

She finally managed to fall into a fitful sleep

filled with nightmares about Custom Pets.

As the sun rose, a cardinal woke Cassie. It was sitting on the tall wooden fence and singing its heart out.

She was so groggy she couldn't remember where she was at first. Then she spotted the bird and the fence, and the hopelessness of her situation came rushing back to her like an avalanche. She was David Ferrante's dog. She had been banished to the backyard for the night because she had muddy paws.

She was still staring at the bird and the tall wooden fence when a new idea began tickling the edges of her mind.

Why didn't I think of it before! she thought. *I'm a dog, so why can't I dig my way out under the fence?* she asked herself in amazement. She cocked her head to one side and sized up the soft dirt along the fence. *It doesn't look like too difficult a job. If I'd started digging last night, I'd be free by now.*

Cassie trotted across the backyard to the corner farthest from the house. Maybe it wasn't too late. No one was up yet in the house.

Finding an extra-soft spot in the dirt, she started digging furiously. Her front paws moved like twin whirlwinds. Dirt flew three feet into the air behind her. Best of all, the hole was quickly getting deeper and deeper.

Cassie knew freedom was on the other side. She would run as fast as she could to her own home. Surely, in some way, she would be able to make her parents understand it was her in this dog body.

Just a little bit farther, and her tunnel would break through to the other side. She was almost there. She could see a tiny pinhole of light. She dug harder and a hole opened up. In another minute she would be able to squeeze through and run for home.

She was so intent on digging that she didn't hear the back door open and Mrs. Ferrante come out onto the porch. And she didn't see the look of shock and horror spread across her face.

"Cassidy!" Mrs. Ferrante screamed. "You're digging up my flower bed! Oh, no. My beautiful flowers are ruined!"

Cassie froze, her paws stretched into the hole and her nose buried in loose dirt.

David and his father had heard the commotion, and now they were outside, too. All three were running across the backyard toward her. She could feel the earth vibrating as if three giant dinosaurs were thundering down on her.

Cassie backed out of the hole. Her tail was tucked firmly between her legs as she desperately looked for a place to hide. She wanted to cry. She had come so close to freedom.

"Come back here, you worthless mutt!" ordered Mr. Ferrante, stomping after her. His fists were clenched. His face was purple with rage. "This is it! The last straw! Finished! You're going back to the pet store right now. And this time I mean it!"

She knew her fate was sealed. Not even David could save her now.

Chapter

With a feeling of dread Cassie climbed into the rear seat of the car. She was going back to Custom Pets. Mr. Willard would be furious when the Ferrantes returned her and demanded their money back. He would take his anger out on her.

Cassie could still see the fat man leering at her through the cage bars. She could hear him threatening to beat her if she didn't stop barking. That had been bad enough. What would he do to her now?

Beside her in the backseat, David hugged her and cried into her fur.

"I'm going to miss you, Cassidy," he said, wiping his nose on the tail of his shirt. "I really *really* am."

To Cassie's surprise she realized she would miss him, too. A little bit, anyway. He wasn't the same obnoxious David she had known at school. The show-off. The troublemaker. The jerk.

He had loved her and had tried to take good care of her. He had even continued to give her food in his napkin when nobody was looking. Saying good-bye to David was going to be harder than she ever would have imagined.

Sighing sadly, she licked his salty face.

Mr. Ferrante found a parking space in front of the pet shop. David led her out of the car and toward the store. Cassie wondered if he could hear her heart beating. Pounding in terror.

She was trembling as they went through the door. She said a silent prayer that Mr. Willard would be gone, replaced by someone kind and gentle with animals. Someone who might be able to help her. Someone who could make her a girl again.

Her heart sank. Mr. Willard had his massive body planted on the stool behind the counter. He looked at them with his watery black eyes when they walked in.

He put down his paperwork and smiled at the Ferrantes.

"Hello, folks. Welcome to Custom Pets. How can I . . ."

His smile faded and his lips set in a hard line as he recognized them. His eyes bulged wider as he glared first at Cassie and then at David's father.

"Something wrong with your dog?" Mr. Willard demanded.

"She's a no-good worthless mutt, that's what's wrong!" snapped Mr. Ferrante.

Cassie's insides were churning as Mr. Willard wheezed and slid off the stool. He came from behind the counter and grabbed the leash from David's hand. Jerking her hard, he hauled Cassie to a cage and forced her inside. Then he slammed the door and locked it.

"Now tell me what the problem is," he said, lumbering across the floor toward David's parents.

David had lingered near the cage. "I'm sorry, Cassidy," he whispered. He reached a hand between the bars to rub her head.

Cassie whimpered softly.

"David!" Mr. Ferrante called. "Get away from that dog right now."

David sighed deeply. "'Bye, Cassidy. I love you." Tears were in his eyes. He wiped them with his shirt-sleeve as he slowly backed away.

Cassie's heart ached as she watched him go. Suddenly, being David's dog didn't seem so bad.

Pacing back and forth in the tiny cage, she

strained to hear what was going on. But they were too far away for her to make out much of the conversation, except for an occasional burst from David's father. "Stupid fleabag." "Barks like an idiot."

Her only hope was that Mr. Willard would refuse to take her back and she could return home with David.

If that happens, I'll never ever bark again, she promised herself. *I'll be the best dog in the world. I'll fetch, and roll over, and bring Mr. Ferrante his paper, and—*

The sudden sound of the cash register slamming shut broke into her thoughts.

"Sorry you folks got a rotten dog," Mr. Willard called out with a hearty laugh. "That happens sometimes. But don't worry. I'll take care of her myself."

Cassie listened in terror as the door closed behind the Ferrantes. Mr. Willard came out from behind the counter and headed toward her.

An evil grin spread across his fleshy face.

M r. Willard stood over Cassie's cage, blocking out what dim light there was in the room. His watery eyes were as cold and hard as a black night. His nostrils widened as his face slowly contorted into an expression of rage.

"So . . . you couldn't handle it, huh?" he asked, sneering. "You had to blow it. Well, we'll just have to do something about that, now, won't we, Cassidy?" His warm, sour breath spread over her like a putrid blanket.

"Let me out of here!" she cried. *"You can't keep me here! I'm a girl, not a dog! And my parents are looking for me. And the police. And if you don't let me out of here, they're going to catch you. And put you in jail!"*

"You can bark your head off, as far as I'm concerned," Mr. Willard said. "It won't do you any good. No one can understand a word you're trying to say. But you already know that, don't you?"

He laughed. It sent chills down Cassie's spine. It made the fur rise on her back.

Cassie backed as far as she could into the corner of her cage. She rolled herself up into a quivering ball and shut her eyes tightly.

She was helpless. Totally at his mercy. She wished she could disappear.

The cage moved and she opened her eyes a slit.

Mr. Willard had picked up the cage. Cradling it against his huge body, he shuffled across the room.

"I think it's time you and I went into the back room," he said with a sinister laugh.

Cassie's heart stopped. *The back room!*

That's where he had taken Cuda.

And that was where the cat had been crying so pitifully.

And that was also the room Mr. Willard had stopped her from entering the day David and his parents ordered a golden retriever.

It was where Mr. Willard had turned her into a dog!

When they reached the door, Mr. Willard balanced the cage on his knee. Digging in his pants pocket, he pulled out a key. He unlocked the door and pushed it open.

Cassie glanced fearfully into the room. It looked like an ordinary storage room. It was filled with cases of dog food, bags of cat litter. All the supplies one would expect to find in the back room of a pet shop. There was also a sink in one corner with a coffeepot on the drain board. Beside the sink was a long table.

Cassie's heart lurched. It reminded her of an examining table she'd once seen in a veterinarian's office.

With a grunt Mr. Willard heaved the cage onto the table. He put his face up close to the bars. His bad breath oozed into the cage.

"I'll bet you'd like for me to turn you back into a girl, wouldn't you, Cassidy?" he asked in a sticky-sweet voice.

Cassie jumped up, wagging her tail furiously, and cried. *"Oh, yes! Yes, please! Oh, please let me be a girl again! I'll never tell anyone what happened here. I promise. Just let me be a girl again!"*

He closed one eye. He had an amused look on his face. "Of course, we both know I couldn't do that, don't we?" he said.

"Yes, you could! You could!" Cassie whined, and gave him a pleading look. Her feet pranced in ex-

101

citement. *"I promise you could! I can keep a secret! I swear!"*

He chuckled softly. "It doesn't do you any good to bark at me that way. Even I can't understand a word you're saying."

Cassie raced around her cage in circles crying, *"You've got to let me out of here! I want to go home!"*

Mr. Willard wheezed deeply. "I suppose there's just one thing to do. Since nobody wants you . . . I'm going to have to put you to sleep."

Chapter

assie watched in horror as Mr. Willard opened the cabinet under the sink. He pulled out a vial of medicine and a syringe.

"It's just a little shot," said Mr. Willard. "It'll hardly hurt at all."

He tipped the medicine vial upside down and stuck the syringe needle into it.

The syringe slowly filled with a clear liquid. Cassie couldn't believe what was happening. She really was going to be put to sleep.

Mr. Willard smiled and hummed to himself as he put down the medicine vial and pointed the syringe upward. He squeezed one lone drop out of the tip of the needle. The poison glistened in the light for an instant. Then it rolled down the shaft of the needle and disappeared.

"Well, Cassidy girl, it looks like everything's ready," he said. "Just relax and be a good dog. There's nothing you can do. You may feel a little sting at first, but it will all be over before you know it."

Was this what had caused the cat's terrible wailing? Cassie wondered.

Fear clogged her throat, choking off her breath. She watched Mr. Willard put the syringe down beside the sink and open the door to her cage. She shrank as far back as she could, but his hand shot inside and grabbed her collar.

A deep growl rose in Cassie's throat. She planted herself firmly, bracing herself against his pull.

He jerked hard on her collar but couldn't budge her.

"I'm warning you!" he snarled angrily. The rolls of fat on his face and neck were turning red. "I'm trying to make this as easy on you as I can."

Cassie growled louder and bared her fangs. Her mind was spinning as his massive hand pulled at her. Veins bulged on his arm just inches from her nose.

"Come *out* of there!" he commanded.

Cassie sank her teeth into his arm as hard as she could.

"Yooowww!" Mr. Willard screamed.

She held on, dangling from his arm as he yanked it out of the cage.

104

"Get off me!" he shrieked, trying to shake her loose.

Cassie dropped to the floor, scrambled to her feet, and raced for the door.

She could hear him cursing behind her.

The door was open a crack. That was all she needed. She could crash through it and into the main part of the store. She would hide somewhere—*anywhere*—until a customer opened the outside door. The final door to freedom . . . and home.

"Come back here, you mangy hound," cried Mr. Willard. "I'll teach you to bite me!"

She heard things being knocked over and his heavy steps behind her. Cassie made a final sprint toward the door.

Suddenly a hand shot out above her and the door slammed shut inches in front of her nose. Unable to stop, Cassie went crashing into it.

Dazed and trembling, she lay by the door.

"Don't think you can get away from me, you stupid mutt." Mr. Willard stood over her, laughing insanely. He held the syringe in one hand. Blood ran down the other and dripped from his fingertips onto the floor.

Cassie knew it was all over.

Chapter 24

Mr. Willard's huge body moved in slow motion. He bent over Cassie. The evil grin on his face chilled her to the bone. Warm blood from his arm splattered onto her coat. He was wheezing hard.

Cassie's eyes opened wide in terror as the syringe full of poison came closer and closer, the tip of the needle nearer and nearer. Mr. Willard's hand reached out to grab her collar again.

Gathering her strength, Cassie jerked away and jumped to her feet.

Mr. Willard lunged for her.

She dashed between his legs and scampered under the examining table, pressing up against the wall.

He let out a yowl of anger.

Bolting upright, Mr. Willard lost control of his immense weight. He fell off balance. He tried grabbing for a stack of dog-food cases to steady himself and dropped the syringe. An instant later he lost his grip and came crashing to the floor.

Mr. Willard lay sprawled out like a giant beached whale.

"Don't think you can outsmart me!" he screamed.

His feet and arms were flailing in the air.

Then he started rolling from side to side like a huge turtle as he tried to get up. "You can't get away!"

Suddenly Cassie spotted the syringe. It was lying on the floor halfway between herself and the bellowing man. She knew what she had to do.

Mr. Willard had managed to get to his hands and knees and was huffing and puffing to catch his breath. Cassie crept out from under the table. She crawled across the floor, keeping an eye on him.

Reaching out a paw, she touched the syringe. It felt ice-cold and evil. It was all she could do to keep from pulling her paw back in horror. But she forced herself not to.

She silently rolled the syringe away from Mr. Willard. She had to hide it, but where? Her heart was beating wildly.

Glancing around quickly, she saw a stack of cat-litter bags in the center of the room. Her paw was trembling as she edged the needle between two of them. Could she push the syringe far enough in between the bags that it would be hidden from sight?

Out of the corner of her eye she could see Mr. Willard struggling to his feet.

Hurry! Hurry! she screamed inside her head.

Using her nose, she pushed the syringe until it was almost out of sight.

Would he see it? She had to draw his attention away! Slinking quickly across the floor on her stomach, Cassie headed for a dark corner. Mops and brooms were leaning against the wall. Maybe she could get behind them. Hide for a little while. Buy herself some time to think. To come up with a plan.

With a gigantic heave Mr. Willard exploded off the floor. He twisted his head first one way and then another, shrieking, "Where are you? I know you're in here somewhere!"

Cassie cringed, shivering behind the cleaning equipment. Mr. Willard was in a wild rage. He stomped around the room, cursing and swiping merchandise onto the floor.

"Come out, you stupid dog! There's no way you can get away from me! *I'm going to get you!*"

He was making his way around the room more slowly now. He was looking behind every box, under every piece of furniture, and into every space big enough for a dog to slip into.

Coming closer and closer to Cassie.

Chapter

Suddenly Mr. Willard spotted Cassie hiding among the mops and brooms. His black eyes glinted brightly as he let out a hideous cackle of delight.

"So . . . my . . . poor . . . little . . . Cassidy. You thought you could get away from me, did you?"

He threw back his head and roared so hard, his body shook like an immense bowl of Jell-O. His laughter echoed off the walls and bounced around the room.

"Well, I've got you now, you mutt," Mr. Willard said, toppling over a stack of dog-food cans that stood in his way. They clattered to the floor.

Cassie peered up at him through the tall handles of the mops and brooms. They closed her into the corner like prison bars. Her teeth were chattering. It felt as if her heart were going to pound its way out of her chest.

"What did you do with my needle?" Mr. Willard demanded. He kicked aside cans and threw a chair out of the way as he advanced toward her. "I know you did something with it. It couldn't have disappeared into thin air."

Cassie fought to keep her eyes on his face. If she looked away, she might accidentally let her eyes linger on the cat-litter bags. Then he'd realize the syringe was hidden there.

Mr. Willard stopped, closed one eye, and studied her for a moment. Then he chuckled.

"Think you're smart, eh?" Waddling across the room, he opened the cabinet below the sink. Bending down, he pulled out the vial of poison and *another syringe*!

Cassie let out a howl. *Owww-wowww-owww.*

"Hah! You didn't think I only had one, did you?" he asked without looking at her. His attention was focused on filling the syringe.

"Be prepared!" he said, laughing. "They taught me that in Boy Scouts. Probably surprises you to know that I was once a Boy Scout, doesn't it?" He giggled crazily to himself.

Then he turned toward Cassie.

With a yelp Cassie exploded through the brooms

and mops, sending them flying in all directions.

She careened around the crowded storage room, dodging through bags of pet food and litter. Under the table and out again, slipping and sliding and scattering cans as Mr. Willard chased her.

She could hear his thundering footsteps.

She felt his doughy hands grabbing at her.

"Stop!" he shouted. "It won't do you any good to run!"

Around and around the room she went, crashing into boxes, scattering a display of dog toys.

Mr. Willard was right behind her, throwing things out of his way.

Cassie leaped over more boxes.

"Stop!" cried Mr. Willard. He was panting and wheezing heavily. "Stop this instant!" he yelled, but his voice was getting fainter. His footsteps slower.

Finally Mr. Willard leaned against the examining table. His huge body was heaving as he gasped for air. His face was glowing bright red from exhaustion. Sweat dripped off the end of his nose. His shirttail was pulled out. His clothes were soaked with perspiration.

With a shaky hand he pulled a handkerchief from his back pocket and mopped his face.

"I said stop!" he tried to cry out again. But his voice was barely above a whisper. His chest was

113

heaving even harder now, and he was holding his side.

Across the room Cassie peered at him from behind a box. Her own breath was coming in ragged gasps. Her tongue was dripping.

What was he going to do now? Was he just pretending to be tired? Was he actually planning another way to trap her?

She looked around quickly. What could she do? *There was no place else to hide!*

Suddenly Mr. Willard shoved himself away from the examining table and stomped to the door. The poison-filled syringe still glinted in his hand.

When he reached the door, he turned around. "I'm going to get help," he wheezed. "And when I get back . . . *you are dead, Cassidy.*"

Chapter

The instant the door slammed behind him, Cassie began pacing back and forth, looking for a place to hide, a way out.

What am I going to do? she screamed inside her head.

She looked around helplessly. Mr. Willard wasn't the only one who was tired. She was exhausted. Her legs trembled so much that she could barely stand. Her head throbbed. Her dry tongue lolled out of the side of her mouth. With help he wouldn't have any trouble catching her and putting her to sleep!

She sagged to the floor to rest a moment and wait until her breathing slowed to normal.

I can't give up! I can't! she told herself stubbornly. *I've got to keep going.*

It took all her energy to struggle to her feet. Frantically she circled the room again, looking for a way out. Hot, thirsty, and desperate, she pushed boxes of dog food away from the wall with her shoulder. She knocked over stacks of cat-food cans and looked under furniture.

It's no use! I'm trapped! she whimpered.

The only door led into the main part of the store, where Mr. Willard was getting help. There was no other way out.

Unless . . .

Cassie looked up.

High up on the wall, near the ceiling, was a tiny window she hadn't noticed before. Dull sunlight was barely able to shine through the grimy pane.

She studied the window for a moment. There was a handle on the bottom near the sill.

Cassie looked down at her paws. *I don't have any fingers!* she moaned. *Even if I could get up to it, I couldn't open it.*

Still, she had to try. She couldn't just stay there and wait for Mr. Willard to come back with help. To come back and put her to sleep.

There was a rickety table beneath the window. On top of it were a few sheets of paper and a fancy cut-glass bottle.

Cassie crouched low and then jumped.

Landing on the table, she slipped on the papers

and scrambled to regain her balance. She held her breath as the table swayed wildly. First to the left and then to the right. Finally it stopped. She breathed a sigh of relief.

Cassie looked up slowly to keep from shaking the table. Her heart sank.

The window was still too far away!

She inched closer to the wall, stopping to steady herself each time the table wobbled.

She pricked up her ears. She froze, listening. What was that sound? Was it Mr. Willard coming back or the table bumping against the floor? Or was it her pounding heart?

Slowly Cassie put her front paws against the wall and stood up on her hind legs. She edged her paws closer and closer to the window.

She stretched upward, straining every muscle. Farther. Farther, until one paw touched the sill.

But she still couldn't reach the handle.

Cassie pressed her tummy against the wall and stood on her toes, stretching as far as she could reach.

Please, she prayed silently, *please let me make it. Only . . . a . . . little . . . bit . . . farther.*

Cassie held her breath as she squeezed out the last bit of stretch she had in her.

She could feel the handle now.

She was touching it!

She tried to wrap her paw around it. Almost. Almost.

Suddenly the table wobbled. Her feet flew out from under her, and she came crashing down.

Oh, no! she cried.

The table swayed wildly, tipping from side to side like a boat in a storm.

Cassie tried to steady it but couldn't.

Suddenly she heard a sickening snap as a table leg broke. The table tilted, sending her sliding and clawing off the edge and down onto the floor.

The fancy cut-glass bottle flew in the air. It landed on the floor and shattered into a million pieces, splattering liquid everywhere.

Cassie lay in a heap, her head resting on the broken table. She looked back up at the window. It might as well be a million miles away.

It's no use! she thought. *He'll be back any minute. I'm finished.*

Sighing deeply, she dropped her head again to await her fate.

She felt a dampness under her chin and rolled her eyes to see what it was. Her big pink tongue was as dry as cardboard.

One last little drink to quench my thirst, she thought. She gently lapped at it, not worrying about drinking in slivers of broken glass. What difference did it make now?

The taste surprised her. *That's good,* she thought, lapping at it again. It was sweet and cool.

When every single bit of the liquid was gone, Cassie stumbled to her feet.

Swaying, she shook her head. She was suddenly dizzy.

She spread her feet to brace herself. The room started spinning. A loud humming noise started in her head.

Cassie tried to take a step, but it was all she could do to move her feet.

She leaned against the wall as sleepiness came rolling over her like giant waves.

I can't resist anymore. I give up. Her mind was almost too groggy to form the thought.

She was falling. Spiraling downward into darkness. But as her eyes closed, she remembered.

Cassie knew in that instant where she had tasted the liquid before!

Chapter

When Cassie opened her eyes, she was sprawled across the floor. The storage room was deathly silent.

She raised her head and listened hard. Nothing. Had something happened to Mr. Willard?

She felt better, stronger. Her heart leaped. Maybe she could still get away!

She pushed herself up onto her hands and knees. *Hands! Knees!*

Cassie gasped and looked down at herself.

Hands! Arms! Legs! Feet! No paws! No furry legs! She looked behind her.

Yessss! No tail!

"I'm a girl again!" she cried in disbelief.

She held her hands up in front of her eyes, wiggling her fingers and giggling.

Next she ran her hands down her long legs. Feet! I've got real girl-type feet! She crossed her eyes to see and gingerly patted her nose, her cheeks, her mouth.

She was normal! She felt giddy.

Cassie threw back her head and laughed out loud.

Then the memories came flooding back.

The sweet-tasting liquid she had lapped off the floor. She remembered now that it was pink! It was the same liquid Mr. Willard had given her when she was turned into a golden retriever.

"Here, drink this. It'll make you feel better," Mr. Willard had said.

She had felt dizzy. Had heard the humming sound. Then everything had gone black.

And when she had awakened . . . she was a dog!

That was how Mr. Willard got his custom pets! He found people who looked like the animals people ordered and changed them with his liquid.

It was impossible, but it had to be true. When she drank the liquid the second time, it changed her back into a girl.

Cassie scrambled to her feet. There was no time to lose. She had no idea how long she had been out.

She looked down at her body.

"Oh, no!" she whispered. "What did he do with my clothes?"

Frantically, Cassie looked in the cabinet under the sink. Nothing.

She looked on shelves and in drawers.

Then she saw a large cardboard box sitting next to the door. She opened it quickly and pulled out shirts, pants, blouses, and shoes. Halfway into the box she found her things. She put them on quickly.

Mr. Willard could come barging in any minute. With help. To put her to sleep.

Would it matter to him that she was a girl again? she wondered. Would it make him change his mind about killing her? Probably not, now that she knew his secret. Especially when he would have a syringe filled with poison in his hand.

Cassie headed for the door and stopped in her tracks. She could hear voices out in the pet shop.

"Back here! Come on!" It was Mr. Willard's voice. She heard footsteps outside the door. "Hurry!"

Whirling around, Cassie dashed for the window. She looked for something to climb up on. The table she had used before was a broken mess.

Frantically she shoved it out of the way and pushed a cart loaded with dog-food cases under the window. She scrambled onto the boxes and reached the window easily!

Grabbing the handle, she tugged hard. The latch didn't give.

Stay cool! she told herself.

She put all her weight on it. This time the latch popped!

Cassie pushed the window open and wiggled through it—at the same time, she heard the store-room door bang open.

She started to run. She ran across the park. Down sidewalks. Around corners. In and out of traffic.

She was *free*!

She was going home!

Chapter

As she ran, Cassie kept looking over her shoulder. Any minute she expected to see Mr. Willard's hulking form lumbering after her. Blood dripping from his arm. The poison-filled syringe held high in his hand.

But as she moved farther and farther away from Custom Pets, she began to relax. Even if he came after her, he'd be looking for a half-grown golden retriever. And he couldn't run that fast or far.

As she turned a corner, Cassie noticed a gray-and-white cat sitting on the branch of a tree. She stopped with a jolt when the cat let out a long, pitiful yowl.

Oh, my gosh, she thought. *That cat sounds just like the one in the back room of Custom Pets.*

Walking to the tree, she peered up at the cat. "Kitty, kitty," she called.

"Meooow," cried the cat.

Cassie swallowed hard. "Are you okay, kitty?" Looking around to make sure no one was near, she added in a whisper, "Are you trying to tell me something? Did you used to be a person?"

The cat blinked its eyes and looked back at her, but it didn't make a sound.

"Wag your tail if the answer is yes," she whispered again.

The cat just stared at her.

Cassie hurried on, feeling a little foolish. At the same time, she couldn't shake the eerie feeling that the cat may have come from Custom Pets. Maybe there were lots of kids like herself who had been turned into animals. What about the other clothes in the box?

Would she be able to tell if she saw an animal from Mr. Willard's store? And would she be able to communicate with it? She had never found out if Cuda had understood her.

A little farther along the street a teenage girl was coming toward her. She was walking a champagne-colored poodle on a leash.

Cassie stared at the dog as it came closer. It had a blue satin bow in its hair. It looked perfectly content as it trotted along beside its mistress. As it got near, it looked at her and let out a little yip.

Have you always been a dog? Cassie wanted to ask. As they passed, the dog looked back at her.

Are you trying to send me a message? Cassie wondered.

All the rest of the way home she kept an eye out for Cuda. *Poor Cuda,* she thought. *I'll bet he was a person and Mr. Willard turned him into a dog.*

But who was he before? she wondered. *Was he my age? I'll try to find him in a day or so,* she promised herself. *At any rate, one thing is certain. I'll never set foot in Custom Pets again!*

Chapter

29

Cassie and her parents talked late into the night. They were so glad to have her home, they believed her story about having amnesia and not knowing where she had been. She knew it was a far-out story, but it was the best she could do. There was no way she could tell them the truth. She could hardly believe what had happened herself.

The next morning was Saturday, and she hurried to the phone to call Suki. She was dying to tell her best friend that she was home.

It seemed like a whole lifetime had passed since she'd last seen Suki. Cassie listened excitedly as the phone rang. One ring. Two rings.

"Come on, Suki," she whispered anxiously. "Be there."

Cassie could scarcely hide her disappointment when Mrs. Chen answered and said that Suki had gone out.

"But she'll be so happy to know that you're home safe and sound," said Mrs. Chen. "I'll have her call you the moment she gets home."

After they hung up, Cassie wandered restlessly around her bedroom. Her mind was filled with disturbing images: Mr. Willard chasing her around the storeroom with the syringe filled with poison. Obedience school and Bruiser. Hunting birds. Eating dog food out of a bowl on the floor. Quadruple yuck!

There was a soft tap on her door.

Her mother called, "Cassie, may your dad and I come in? We have a little surprise for you."

"Sure," said Cassie, swinging the door open for them.

Her mouth dropped open, and she gasped with pleasure when she saw what her mother was holding.

"A dog!" she cried. "Isn't she cute. Whose is she? Where did she come from?"

"She's yours, sweetheart," said her dad. "She's a Pekingese, and we knew you'd love her."

"While you were missing, we talked over our objections to a pet. We decided we were being overprotective," said her mother. She put the fluffy little

130

dog in Cassie's outstretched arms. "We knew how badly you wanted a dog, so we went to a pet shop a few minutes ago and got her for you. We hope you like her."

Cassie took the squirming bundle of fur in her arms. The little dog's eyes were sparkling. She licked Cassie on the cheek and then hopped out of her arms, barking a high-pitched little bark.

"Thanks, Mom. Thanks, Dad. She's beautiful, and I love her already."

As soon as her parents left her room, Cassie knelt to the floor beside her new pet.

"You are absolutely the *cutest* dog I've ever seen!" she said. "I'll have to think of a perfect name for you."

The little dog was a bundle of energy. She bounced up and down and raced around and around the room.

Cassie bent double with laughter. "You're so funny! You remind me of my best friend, Suki."

Suddenly the little dog stopped running. It looked up at Cassie with pleading eyes. Then without warning it turned a perfect back flip.

Cassie stopped cold and stared at the dog.

"Suki!?"

itz Traflon scowled into the trash can. Running across the top of the junk inside was a giant brown cockroach. Fitz held the empty peanut-butter jar directly over it.

"Bombs away! *Boom!*" he said as he dropped the jar.

He picked up the jar and looked under it. The cockroach's antennae were still moving, so he squashed it.

Most of his buddies were fascinated by bugs, but not Fitz. He hated them.

He picked up the peanut-butter-and-jelly sandwich he had been making and stuffed it into his bulging backpack. With his luck, it would be squashed, just like the cockroach, by lunchtime. A brown-and-purple gooey mess.

"I can't believe it's my twelfth birthday *and* the first day of school. What a *rotten* way to spend my birthday."

Fitz trudged out of the house and down the sidewalk. He was thinking about all his other birthdays.

They had each fallen a day or two before the start of school. They had been *fun*! Parties with cake and presents and all his friends. Trips to the water park or the zoo. Never before in his life had his birthday fallen on the crummy first day of school.

He was still grumbling to himself when he arrived at Maple Grove Middle School. He stopped on the sidewalk and looked at the two-story red-brick building. It looked just like it had last year.

Like a prison.

Fitz sighed and shoved his hands in his pockets. He hated school. Same old stuff year after year. Except each year it got harder. He had hoped all summer that school would be different this year.

Fun, maybe.

Different, at least.

Obviously he was going to be out of luck.

"Hey, Fitz! Guess what?"

He looked around to see Sarah Cherone and Lexi Palmer rushing toward him.

Oh, no. Not those two, Fitz thought.

They were giggling and gushing.

"Hi, Fitz," said Sarah. She batted her eyelashes at him the way she always did. It was disgusting. Then she and Lexi giggled again.

"Hi," he mumbled.

"You're never going to believe this," Lexi went on breathlessly. "Tell him, Sarah."

"Yeah, Fitz. Our school has a new cook!"

"Big deal," he replied. "Who cares about a crummy cook?"

"You will when you see her," Lexi assured him. "This cook is seriously weird."

"Her name's Miss Larva Webb, and she's got—" Sarah went on, but Fitz tuned her out.

He couldn't stand to listen to her. She bugged him all the time. Fitz hated all girls, but he hated Sarah the most.

"Hey, Traflon. Over here."

Brian's voice cut into Fitz's thoughts.

"What's up?" he called as he hurried toward Brian.

"Have I ever got something to show you," Brian said excitedly.

"What is it?" Fitz asked as he trotted beside his best friend.

"You'll see," said Brian.

"Hey, Brian. What's the big mystery? Come on, tell me," Fitz insisted.

"You've got to see it yourself to believe it," said Brian.

The moment Fitz realized they were heading toward the cafeteria, he tugged on Brian's sleeve. "This doesn't have anything to do with the new cook, does it?" he asked.

Brian nodded. "Wait 'til you see her."

"Come on, Brian," Fitz insisted. "Give me a break. What's the big deal about a cook?"

Brian pushed open the double doors to the lunchroom and shoved Fitz in. He pulled Fitz down behind a table and pointed toward the cook who was polishing the empty steam tables with a cloth.

Fitz rolled his eyes in exasperation. He'd seen cooks before. Lots of them. And this one didn't look that different. She was an older lady with white curly hair. She was wearing a white apron, and a tall chef's hat was perched on her head. The strangest thing about her that Fitz could see was the large dark sunglasses she was wearing.

"She looks pretty normal to me, except for the glasses," Fitz whispered.

Suddenly he did a double take.

The cook was wearing a weird-looking necklace. It was a chain with lots of little baubles hanging from it.

He frowned. "Am I seeing things?" he whispered, squinting at the necklace. The baubles seemed to be moving.

Fitz raised his head so that he could see better. His eyes flew open in alarm. The baubles on her necklace were *bugs*.

And they were alive!